W9-BXR-506

SECRET

OF THE

STORM

ALSO BY BETH MCMULLEN

Mrs. Smith's Spy School for Girls
Mrs. Smith's Spy School for Girls
Power Play
Double Cross

Lola Benko, Treasure Hunter
Lola Benko, Treasure Hunter
The Midnight Market

SECRET OF THE STORM

Beth McMullen

ALADDIN

New York   London   Toronto   Sydney   New Delhi

❤ **ALADDIN**

An imprint of Simon & Schuster Children's Publishing Division
1230 Avenue of the Americas, New York, New York 10020
First Aladdin hardcover edition March 2022
Text copyright © 2022 by Beth McMullen
Jacket illustration copyright © 2022 by Vivienne To
All rights reserved, including the right of reproduction in whole or in part in any form.
ALADDIN and related logo are registered trademarks of Simon & Schuster, Inc.
For information about special discounts for bulk purchases, please contact
Simon & Schuster Special Sales at 1-866-506-1949 or business@simonandschuster.com.
The Simon & Schuster Speakers Bureau can bring authors to your live event. For more information or to book an event contact the Simon & Schuster Speakers Bureau
at 1-866-248-3049 or visit our website at www.simonspeakers.com.
Designed by Laura Lyn DiSiena
The text of this book was set in Chaparral Pro.
Manufactured in the United States of America 0122 FFG
10 9 8 7 6 5 4 3 2 1
Library of Congress Cataloging-in-Publication Data
Names: McMullen, Beth, 1969– author.
Title: The secret of the storm / Beth McMullen.
Description: First Aladdin hardcover edition. | New York : Aladdin, 2022. | Series: The Albert project ; book 1 | Audience: Ages 8 to 12. | Summary: Cassie King's father has died, her mother has retreated into herself, away from reality, and her best friend has abandoned her for the in crowd, so when she and her sort-of friend, Joe, find a kitten during an intense electrical storm, Cassie is determined to adopt him; but Albert (named for Einstein) is no ordinary kitten: he is incredibly strong, things around him tend to burn, his eyes glow red, and when he gets annoyed, the weather turns dangerous—in fact, Albert is a dragon, and there is someone searching for him with very unfriendly intentions.
Identifiers: LCCN 2021028100 (print) | LCCN 2021028101 (ebook) |
ISBN 9781534482852 (hardcover) | ISBN 9781534482876 (ebook)
Subjects: LCSH: Kittens—Juvenile fiction. | Dragons—Juvenile fiction. | Magic—Juvenile fiction. | Mothers and daughters—Juvenile fiction. | Friendship—Juvenile fiction. | CYAC: Cats—Fiction. | Dragons—Fiction. | Magic—Fiction. | Mothers and daughters—Fiction. | Friendship—Fiction.
Classification: LCC PZ7.1.M4644 Se 2022 (print) | LCC PZ7.1.M4644 (ebook) |
DDC 813.6 [Fic]—dc23
LC record available at https://lccn.loc.gov/2021028100
LC ebook record available at https://lccn.loc.gov/2021028101

IN MEMORY OF MY BROTHER DAVID VON ANCKEN.
AND FOR MEG LONDON-BOCHE,
FOR WHOM I AM SO VERY GRATEFUL.

CONTENTS

Chapter 1

HOW IT BEGINS

THE WIDE HALLWAYS of Washington Middle School are no joke. Lives are made in these hallways, or ruined. Last week, for example, someone smeared superglue on Trevor Addison's locker handle, and he was stuck fast. The janitor showed up with a blowtorch. Things quickly got out of hand.

My best friend, Mia Wilson, said Trevor probably deserved it, which I definitely didn't agree with, because no one deserves to be superglued to a locker, but I kept that opinion to myself. Lately, Mia finds everything I say exasperating or wrong, even something as straight up as "good morning." We once promised to be best friends forever, but I'm starting to think she's had a change of heart.

Usually, we meet on the sidewalk outside of school and walk home together, but the last few days she's left without me. She says I'm too slow getting out of school and she needs to get home and change for soccer practice. Sure, sometimes I'm late because Mrs. Holmes, my science teacher, wants to talk about a new recycling strategy they are using successfully in Australia or wherever, and I have to stay for that conversation because saving the planet is *important*. I mean, without it we are in serious trouble. Plus, I like Mrs. Holmes. She encourages me to share my ideas, but mostly I don't because even if I have the perfect answer in my head, I'm not that good at actually saying it out loud. It always comes out sounding weird. Or wrong. Or not what I meant.

But today is different. Determined not to let Mia down, I plan to get myself to the sidewalk exactly on time, no matter what. My dad once told me the universe was on my side. All I had to do was try hard and I could *make* things happen.

"You just can't quit, Cassie," he said. "The universe doesn't like quitters."

When the final bell of the day rings, students spill from classrooms like a great surge of water bursting through a dam. I avoid eye contact with Mrs. Holmes, slipping out with the rush. I race to my locker and check for glue. All clear. And the locker doesn't even jam when I try to open it. This is a good omen. Things are looking up. Right? Stuffing my books into my backpack, I bolt for the exit without even zipping the bag. I'm pretty sure my math textbook falls out, but I don't stop. I'm on a mission. The universe doesn't like quitters.

Outside, a cold Lewiston wind whips the fog into little cyclones that swirl and eddy like ballet dancers. Lewiston is not what people think of when they think of California. There are no palm trees, no movie stars, no sun-drenched beaches dotted with surfers looking to catch the next perfect wave.

Squished between dense mountains and a craggy ocean shoreline, basically in the middle of nowhere, Lewiston is a university town so far up the California coast that we might as well be in Oregon. Even super-boring Sacramento is hundreds of miles away. It rains constantly, and when it's not raining, it's foggy, and when it's not foggy, it's just plain gray. On the rare occasion when the sun *does* come out, Lewiston sparkles like the Emerald City, with trees a hundred shades of green coming right to the edge of an endless blue sea. But it never lasts, the sun, and those moments only remind us of what we are missing.

More importantly, nothing interesting ever happens in

Lewiston. Like, *ever*. If you look up "boring" in the dictionary, there will be a picture of Lewiston.

Strands of brown frizzy hair cling to my eyelashes, blinding me. I clear the hair just in time to see Mia glide out of school, surrounded by the Popular Posse, girls who last year did not know she existed. She wears a new down jacket, the color of a pineapple, that I have never seen before. The Popular Posse moves in a tight bunch, like an amoeba, giggling and whispering and oozing confidence all over everything. I shelter behind a row of pines and try to pull my tangled mess of hair into a ponytail. If I look like I just got electrocuted, Mia will say something snarky about the frizz or my uniform of leggings and hoodies, and that tight, uncomfortable feeling in my stomach will show up and stay for the rest of the day. The girls drift toward me, chattering like monkeys, and I'm about to step out and wave when I hear my name. There is something in the tone that stops me fast.

"Cassie Jones," says Sadie, a girl with sleek black hair where no strand would dare be out of place. "I mean, *why*? Does she even ever *speak*?"

"Seriously," concurs Lila, brand-new phone tucked casually into the pocket of her shredded skinny jeans. "She's the opposite of fun."

"And her clothes?" adds Ruth, puckering up a questioning, lip-glossy pout. "I mean, tall and dorky is not a good look. Target would be an upgrade."

My heart snaps against my ribs. I can't catch my breath. Surely, Mia will defend me. She'll set them straight, tell them we shouldn't judge someone's worth based on appearance, and we'll walk home together, and everything will be fine. Everything will be like it's always been. Right?

"I firmly believe things happen for a reason," Mia explains seriously to her new friends. "Obviously, Cassie's situation was meant to get me to reexamine who I was spending my time with."

There are murmured agreements. Well, of course, *obviously*.

My cheeks burn with shame as I attempt to disappear into the trees. And really, what Dad said about trying hard isn't true. The universe doesn't care if I quit. It is a cold, empty, bleak place, and it doesn't care about me *at all*. If I fade to nothing, it will not notice.

Keeping my head down, I slink away, vanishing among the groups of friends, all laughing and going places and having fun. The wind is blowing so hard my eyes water.

But I'm not crying.

Chapter 2

GRAVITATIONALLY COMPLETELY COLLAPSED OBJECTS, AKA BLACK HOLES

WHEN I BURST THROUGH THE DOORS of the Lewiston Public Library, where I volunteer after school, the librarian, Miss Asher, looks alarmed. "Cassie," she says, rushing out from behind the formidable main desk, "what on earth happened to you?"

"Nothing," I sniffle. "It's just really cold out. And windy."

"Well, that's just Lewiston in November," she says. "And every other month." She hustles me behind the mega-desk and wraps a fuzzy purple blanket around my shoulders. She keeps a pile of blankets on hand because the building is ancient and the heating often goes on the fritz. It's actually the oldest building in the city of Lewiston. Lewiston

University was founded right here in 1890, and I swear they have done nothing to update it since.

Miss Asher tucks the blanket around me like I'm an upright burrito. "That's better," she says, smiling. Miss Asher has short spiky hair, dyed a rainbow of colors, and a tattoo of a cat on the back of her neck. She wears faded jeans, heavy black boots, and friendship bracelets up to her elbow. A tiny stud in her nose is the aquamarine of a tropical ocean. She is exactly eighteen years, two months, and six days older than I am and was my mother's student at Lewiston Senior High School.

And sometimes I think Miss Asher can see into my brain. Without comment, she hands me the giant plastic bin of Twizzlers she keeps stashed in the desk. She has a sixth sense about days when Twizzlers are necessary. "No Mia today?" she asks.

I gag a little on my licorice. "No. I think she has practice." It's Tuesday. She doesn't have practice, and even though Miss Asher is my favorite person in the world and the library is the only place where I feel as if I can exhale, I can't bring myself to tell her what just happened in front of the school. *Target would be an upgrade. Cassie's situation.*

"Too bad," Miss Asher says, sorting some papers on her research desk. There is a man, tall, thin, and wearing a puffy orange jacket, standing at Miss Asher's desk, impatiently waiting for her attention while she ignores him. Library patrons stand at Miss Asher's desk all the time, but not many of them look like the modern version of Dracula. I startle when he turns his pale eyes and angular face in my direction. A thin fringe of hair rings his head, small but pronounced tufts at his ears.

But it's really the teeth that are the problem. Unusually pointy incisors dig into his lower lip, pulling what might be a smile into a grimace. This man is probably the same age as Miss Asher. Or he could be one thousand years old. If we are talking vampires, it's hard to say.

"Excuse me," the man interrupts. "But we were in the middle of a conversation."

Miss Asher, who is nice and understanding to every single person on the planet, shoots him a hot glare I have never seen before. "No, Sheldon," she says tightly. "We were *not* in the middle of anything. This obsession of yours will ruin your life. You're even risking your job. The university is not going to keep looking the other way. And what is it all for? Cyrus is *gone*. You need to move on."

"But the *storm*," he insists, stomping his foot like an angry little kid. "It's happening just as Edward said it would. Why are you pretending it's not? This could change *everything.*" Clearly, I've wandered into something. At least it is distracting me from my Mia problems. I gnaw on a Twizzler and wait to see what happens next.

"Listen to me, Sheldon," Miss Asher says. "When was the last time you visited your parents? You spend all your time searching for a clue or an answer or whatever that doesn't *exist.* Do you even remember *why* you are doing this?"

"Of course," Sheldon says, indignant.

"Then tell me," Miss Asher presses.

Sheldon's face strains with anger, like he's about to burst. "To prove I'm *right*," Sheldon hisses. But just as quickly, he realizes he has fallen into Miss Asher's verbal trap and tries to backpedal. "And to save people from pain and suffering."

"You've completely scrambled the means and the ends," Miss Asher says slowly. "In the beginning it was about Cyrus, and now it's about *you.* Go home, Sheldon. I don't want to talk about this anymore."

The Sheldon vampire-guy stands stock-still, lips parted slightly, eyes narrowed. I suspect he has a rebuttal to Miss Asher's statement, but he does not deliver it. Instead he turns on his heel and leaves without a word. Miss Asher brings her attention back to me as I busily stuff my face with one Twizzler after another.

"Who was that?" I ask.

"An old friend," she says with a heavy sigh. "But no one really. Nothing to worry about." Well, not until the sun goes down, anyway. I mean, those *teeth*.

"Oh, did I mention that Joe is coming today?" Miss Asher adds. "He can help you while Mia is at practice."

Wait a minute. Did she say "Joe"? As in Joe Robinson, the most annoying human at Washington Middle School, who compulsively tells stories that cannot possibly be true? Isn't my bad day bad enough already? Apparently not, because on cue, Joe Robinson flies into the library. A baseball cap sits askew on his close-cropped hair, dark eyes barely visible behind fogged-up glasses. A gray Washington Middle hoodie comes down to his knees, under which he wears shorts, despite the weather, exposing his thin brown legs. Honestly, it's a little surprising the wind didn't blow him to Oz.

Joe is the youngest of five kids and the odd one out. His big brothers are either wildly popular, egghead smart, sporty, or a triple threat. Of course, Joe's nickname is "runt." If Joe were less annoying, I might feel sorry for him.

"Hi, Joe," Miss Asher says with a wave. "Cassie's here, too."

At the mention of my name, Joe's face lights up. "Cassie. Excellent." In addition to being annoying, Joe Robinson is also a self-proclaimed computer genius. He swears he can hack any system in the world. Naturally, this outrageous claim led to epic-level mockery by his classmates. Considering how harsh some of the kids were, Joe took it very well. He never once cried or complained.

But funny things started to happen to his chief tormentors. Their laptops were infected with nasty viruses. Their social media accounts began posting random and embarrassing photos. Student projects disappeared from the school network. Phones refused to charge. Data vanished. A particularly mean boy ended up on the FBI's Most Wanted list, and I'm not even kidding. The photo used was age enhanced, and the list of crimes was long and detailed, including the theft of a valuable Persian kitten, a truly despicable crime.

After that, the bullies steered clear of Joe. But so did everybody else, as if he had a dangerous superpower he could unleash at any moment. Even his brothers pretended he didn't exist. After school, Joe takes care of the library computers because he likes Miss Asher, and also because he has nowhere else to go. Kind of like me.

"Hi, Cassie." Joe dumps his heavy backpack right at my feet and sits down. Without asking, he snatches the bin of Twizzlers out of my lap.

"Hey!" I protest.

"Hay is for horses," he snickers.

"Whatever."

"That's not a very good comeback. I expect more from you, Cassie. Something *clever.*"

"Whatever times two." I shrug off the blanket, warm enough now to start my job of shelving books. But before I can make a clean getaway, Joe asks, "Did you know that NASA finally got a photograph of a black hole? I remember you like them. Black holes, I mean. From science class. You raised your hand to ask about the time thing."

This catches me off guard. I know exactly what he's talking about because I *never* raise my hand in class. Dad once said that I need to learn not to be afraid of my own voice, but the truth remains: when I speak in class, it's a big deal—for me, anyway. But why does Joe remember? It was two months ago. "You did ask about the event horizon, didn't you?"

Well. Yeah. Apparently, if you go beyond the event horizon (that's the point at which everything is sucked into a black hole), time ceases to exist. Try as I might, I just couldn't wrap my head around this concept. I found it so perplexing, I actually raised my hand to ask for clarification. "If time can stop," I blurted at the teacher, "can it also rewind or fast-forward or skip around? Does it mean reality is shaped like a coiled spring? Is it possible to travel from point to point in a nonlinear fashion?"

"Ha! Like you're going to invent a time machine." The blond boy sitting next to me snickered and elbowed his buddy. "She's nonlinear in her brain." The Popular Posse seated behind me giggled. Did Mia giggle with them? I kept my eyes pinned on the teacher.

Hushing the students, the teacher tried gallantly to clear up my confusion, but the concept still felt wildly beyond my grasp. To be honest, I still don't get it. But that does not explain why Joe remembers this particular incident in science class.

"You're right," I admit, flushing at the memory of my humiliation. "I did ask." And in case you were wondering, I *never* said anything about a time machine.

"I like black holes too." Joe stands. He's four inches shorter than I am. I can see the price tag dangling off the top of his new hat. "Anything in space, really. The vast great unknown." He nudges the blanket with his toe. "The photographs won't be available to the public for a while, but I can probably show them to you now. If you want."

Hold on a minute. Didn't he just say the public can't view them yet? My pulse quickens. "You can do that?"

"I have ways." He shrugs. "Besides, it's just NASA."

Just NASA? I narrow my gaze. Is this *just* another one of Joe's wild stories? Do I believe him? Joe shifts uncomfortably in his sneakers. I have work to do, books that need attention. Plus, Mia hates Joe because her phone was among those that mysteriously would no longer charge and had to be replaced. And things are bad enough with her already. I should say no. But the temptation of seeing a real, actual black hole, in which time does not happen, overwhelms everything else.

"Fine," I challenge. "Show me."

As we make our way to the computer room, Joe regales me with tales of skateboarding down Hudson Street. "I had a five percent chance of success, but I kicked butt," he says. "Or at least I didn't fall on it." I don't believe a word of his story. Hudson Street happens to be the steepest in Lewiston, careening out of the mountains right through the center of town, and if he really rode down it, he wouldn't be here in the library. He'd be on a slab at the morgue. He only shuts up when finally seated at the computer, his fingers dancing with precision over the gray keyboard. I think he hums a tune, but he might just be burping.

There's a reason time ceasing to exist as we know it

appeals to me. Time marches forward no matter what we do. But what if we could manipulate time, jump it forward or backward or surf reality however we want? And if that's possible, what is to stop me from returning to the exact moment twelve months, fourteen days, eight hours, and thirty-seven minutes ago when a random man fell asleep at the wheel of his car and struck my father while he was crossing the street?

I could *save* him. And everything would go back to the way it used to be, back when it all made sense.

Chapter 3

INFINITY

JOE TAPS AWAY MERRILY on the computer, humming or burping, while I shift my weight nervously from foot to foot. If whatever Joe is doing is illegal, and I'm pretty sure it is, I really wish he'd hurry. A bead of sweat forms on my eyebrow despite the chill. My mouth is dry. I glance over my shoulder when a library patron drifts into the computer room, but she seems uninterested in us.

"Hurry up," I urge.

"This is not *uncomplicated*," Joe shoots back. I kick myself for being impatient. I could have just waited to see the photographs when they are released to the rest of the world. Any second now a squad of black-suited agents from

Homeland Security or the FBI or whoever is in charge of these things is going to burst through the doors and arrest us. I gnaw on a cuticle. Days go by. At this pace I'm going to run out of cuticles. And possibly fingers.

Finally Joe claps his hands and grins triumphantly. "Here you go. A black hole. As promised."

Being that I'm the kind of person who does not raise her hand in class, Joe has every right to be surprised when I hip check him out of his seat for a better view of the image on the monitor. It turns out a black hole looks like a glowing orange doughnut with blurred edges, resting on a black sheet of paper. The orange on the bottom half of the doughnut is much brighter than the top.

"Wow," I stammer. "That's really it?" I guess he was telling the truth about his hacking abilities, not that I ever actually doubted them.

"Yup. First image ever. It took eight radio telescopes from around the world to capture it." Joe goes on with the details, but I'm not listening. I stare at the black hole, sure I can see the razor edge of the event horizon. The *actual* event horizon, right there in black and white. Well, black and orange, but whatever, the idea makes my skin tingle.

"What do you think?" Joe asks, examining my face.

"It's cool." But that's not the half of it. It thrills me

right down to my tennis shoes. My hands shake. It makes me believe that anything is possible, that things we cannot see or understand still exist. The world seems much bigger than it did five minutes ago. "Thanks for sharing it with me."

Joe glows. "You're welcome."

"Kids?" It's Miss Asher, striding toward us. Joe smacks the keyboard, and the image vanishes. I spring to my feet. Nothing to see here. "Joe, I need you at the printer. It's exploding ink, and it got all over a patron, and, well, it's turned into kind of a situation."

"On it." Joe follows Miss Asher out of the computer room, and I flop back in the chair, the image of the black hole taking up all the space in my brain. My face feels funny, stretched somehow, and I realize I'm smiling.

Two hours later, books shelved, I collect my backpack and say goodbye to Miss Asher, who stands behind the reference desk, gazing into the far away. Like, over-the-rainbow far away. At least the vampire is nowhere in sight. She clutches a pale yellow spiral notebook with a strange colorful symbol sketched on the front.

"What's that?" I ask, pointing to the notebook. The sketched symbol looks like a medieval cathedral stained glass window, like something I should recognize, although I can't say why.

Miss Asher's eyes widen as she abruptly returns to the here and now. "Oh! I didn't see you there, Cassie." She looks down at the notebook in her hands, surprised to find it there. "This old thing? It's nothing. Just . . . something from a long time ago." And she stuffs the notebook into the top right-hand drawer of the desk, the one that is always locked, the one where I'm convinced she hides the really good candy. You know, like the king-sized Snickers bars and giant bags of M&M's that she does not want to share. I can't say I blame her.

"Back tomorrow?" Miss Asher asks. The key to the drawer is on a chain that she slips over her head.

"Yup," I reply. What else am I going to do? Work on my time machine? Seeing the black hole was amazing— mind-blowing, even—but remembering that moment in science class was *not*. That's what I get for opening my mouth. No wonder Mia doesn't want to hang out with me.

As Miss Asher gives me a hug, I catch a whiff of citrus and shampoo. I always try to breathe extra deeply when she hugs me so I can take some of her along when I go. "I'll see you tomorrow," she says. "Stay warm!"

When I step outside into the wind, I'm surprised to find Joe sitting on one of the benches outside the entrance, holding his hat on his head. His hands are covered in blue ink. Even his fingernails are tinted. As I navigate around him, he jumps to his feet. "Hey. I thought we could walk home and talk some more about black holes."

Being spotted with Joe in the library is risky enough, but out here on the street, pretty much anyone could see us. It's about a twenty-minute walk to my house from the library. The route cuts through downtown Lewiston, a tidy grid of streets hosting a collection of coffeehouses, burger joints, pizza places, and bubble tea shops. Miss Asher says this is because we are a college town and coffee, pizza, burgers, and bubble tea are what college students want. I'm about to say no to Joe's offer of walking together when I catch the look in his eyes, and my answer sticks fast in my throat. Maybe the weather is so lousy, everyone will be inside and no one will see us.

"Sure," I croak. "We can walk." And this way I can grab his ankle if a strong gust of wind tries to carry him away. Miss Asher would certainly appreciate that. Joe launches into a moment-by-moment reenactment of his heroic attempts to stop the ink geyser, which he claims was 80 percent successful. Although now that he really thinks about it, it was possibly closer to 75. There was collateral damage. The library patron's favorite Hawaiian shirt was ruined.

A few minutes later, we turn down the alley behind Buddy's Best Burgers. The alley smells like a grease fire but is a shortcut around the intersection with the streetlights that take forever to change. It's also a wind tunnel, the howling concentrated to an unbearable pitch.

Joe stops to adjust his hat, which is determined to fly away. Hunched over, leaning into the wind, we look like two turtles, overstuffed backpacks as our protruding shells. For whatever reason, this makes me laugh. The sound erupts like lava and feels so weird that I want it to stop, but just glancing at Joe the turtle sets me off again.

"What's so funny?" Joe squints into the wind. "The ink was a disaster, a total catastrophe. It almost got on my eyeballs. I might have gone blind."

"You look like a turtle," I yell, clutching my chest, breathless. "I mean, *we* look like turtles."

"What?" Joe shouts. "Hurdles?"

"No! Turtles!" The blue dumpster pushed up against Buddy's back wall stinks, and escaped burger wrappers dance wildly in the air. One of them smacks me in the face. Gross.

"Did you say curtains?" Oh boy. I wipe the tears from

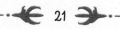

my cheeks and wave off a confused Joe. There is no point in talking until we leave the alley. I motion for Joe to get going. He squares his shoulders and presses into the wind. And just as we pass the blue dumpster, at that exact moment, things take a sharp right turn into completely weird.

Chapter 4

AN ATMOSPHERIC EVENT

THE AIR SNAPS WITH ELECTRICITY and the acrid funk of melting plastic. "What the heck?" I yell. But my words are drowned out by a sharp crack. A perfect zigzag lightning bolt slams into the dumpster, sending it five feet in the air, as if weightless. It lands with an awful crash. A jolt runs from my feet through the top of my head. Joe yelps and leaps behind me, burying his face in my backpack. He might be screaming. My skin prickles in the charged air. The dumpster glows red hot.

"Cassie!"

"It's okay!" I shout. But really it's not. Pressure bears down from above, like a powerful ocean wave pushing us to the sandy bottom. Hail, the size of golf balls, rains from the sky. I hold an arm above our heads against the assault as we huddle close to the back wall of Buddy's Best Burgers. The temperature plummets as the hail smashes the scorching dumpster, sizzling and popping, a splash of water in a hot frying pan. My pulse races.

"It's an atmospheric event!" Joe yells in my ear.

A what? And more importantly, when is it going to *end*? The wind howls. Joe keeps his eyes squeezed shut, still clinging desperately to my backpack. My dad was always saying how much he loved the climate in Lewiston, the mossy, damp smell, the constant drizzle keeping everything green and alive, the moody fog. But *this* was not what he was talking about. The noise crescendos.

And then, abruptly, as if some weather god flipped a switch, the storm stops. The wind dies down and the temperature returns to normal cold, wet Lewiston. But the intense burned-plastic smell lingers. I poke Joe in the bicep.

"You can look now. It's over."

"Really?" He doesn't open his eyes, and he doesn't let go of me. "Are you sure?"

"Pretty sure."

He squints with one eye and scans the alley. Everything looks exactly as it did five minutes ago, before we were almost turned into human French fries. I shake free of Joe and stand up on wobbly legs. Joe works his way to his feet, back pressed firmly against the wall for support.

"The dumpster," he whispers. "Was it . . . glowing?"

I nod. Had I been alone in the alley, I would have assumed my mind was playing tricks on me because, well . . . *weird*. But Joe saw the red-hot dumpster too.

"I am one hundred percent freaked out," he adds.

"What did you say this was?" I ask.

"An atmospheric event." He rolls the tension out of his shoulders and shakes out his arms and legs as if we are in gym class. When I look at him blankly, he sighs. "A weather anomaly. An unusual occurrence. A rarity. Random lightning and giant hail in Lewiston? I mean, we only get two kinds of weather: raining and raining."

I hold up my hand for him to stop. "Okay. I get it."

But he is captivated by my feet. "Your sneakers," he whispers. I am well aware that they are a little worn and definitely not fashion forward, but does he really want to discuss that *now*? "Look."

I glance down to see that the rubber soles of my sneakers have melted and are cooling into a lumpy mess. Joe's shoes have suffered the same fate. We stare at our feet and at each other.

"I think our soles saved our, you know, *souls* from the lightning." Joe gulps. "Part of me is freaking out, and part of me thinks this is really, like, cool."

"Same."

"Do you think anyone else saw what we saw?" Joe asks.

The alley is empty. There is no evidence that anything happened beyond our shoes. And I'm not one of those people who manages to catch every interesting thing that ever happens on video, mostly because I do not own a phone. This experience is mine and Joe's alone. "I don't think so."

We stand in awkward silence for a moment, thinking about what to do next. "We should get going," Joe says finally.

"Yeah." But walking on our mangled shoes is no easy thing. We sway this way and that, unable to keep our balance. That I hear the sound at all over Joe's giggling is a surprise. It's so faint, for a moment I think I imagined it, like it happened in my head. The words "stuck" and "help" flash bright in my mind, but they are fragments, attached to no larger thought.

I grab Joe's arm to stop him. "Wait. Do you hear something?"

"What? No."

"Listen." There it is again. A tiny little *meow*. "A cat."

Joe shakes his head. "Maybe your brain got fried?"

"Quiet." I follow the sound back down the alley, right to the gross big blue dumpster. The meowing grows louder and more insistent, as if the tiny creature responsible knows I'm out here.

"Oh, *now* I hear it," Joe says.

"It's in the dumpster."

"But it was just a thousand degrees. It got hit by lightning! There is no way any living thing could survive the glowing, smoking hot dumpster of death." Joe waves his arms around like a windmill. *"Not* possible!"

"Whatever," I say. "Help me get it open."

The metal is still hot to the touch as we heave up the lid, releasing a terrible stink. Joe gags and turns away. "Aww, this is worse than a corpse flower," he moans. "They smell like a rotting corpse, in case you were wondering."

"I wasn't, but thanks." Burying nose and mouth in my sleeve, I peer inside. The dumpster is full of smoldering Buddy's garbage, half-eaten gray burgers, limp leftover fries, pieces of bun crusted with ketchup. Puffs of smoke rise up, but there are no *actual* flames. My eyes water. "Hello in there."

In the back corner, a tiny black kitten, fur sticky with

some unknown goo, struggles to get out from under a small cardboard box. His paws are no bigger than pennies, and his fuzzy ears strain forward with the effort. But he's too small, and the box is too big, and he slips back behind it. Joe appears at my shoulder.

"What is it?"

"It's a cat," I say.

"No way. Not possible. Not. Not. Not."

"It's a kitten. But he's stuck." The kitten pops his little head up above the box and fixes his green eyes on me, and I feel a shock as vivid and intense as when the lightning passed through me not ten minutes ago and melted my sneakers. And without a second thought, I hoist myself up onto the lip of the dumpster.

Naturally, Joe is concerned. "Are you *crazy*? You can't go in there! It's on fire! You'll burn. And the smell! Did you not hear the thing about the corpse flower?" His breathing is fast and sharp. He's losing it. But those green eyes hold me hostage. I have no choice but to get in the dumpster and rescue this kitten.

"It's fine," I explain calmly. "Just a tiny bit hot. Hold on, little peanut. I'm coming."

"I *cannot* believe you are doing this," Joe cries, burying his face in his hands. "There's a one hundred percent chance you come out completely gross and possibly dead."

"I won't die," I mutter. "And I'll take a shower." Swinging my legs over the edge, I hop down into the garbage. It's like walking on a recently extinguished campfire, each step sending up little puffs of ash. But really, my worry about the fire is overwhelmed by the smell, so much worse than a corpse flower on the inside. I sway a little as bile works its way up my throat.

"Cassie! Are you going to pass out? Do you need me to come in there with you? I really don't want to, but I will."

All things considered, that might be the nicest thing anyone has said to me in a long time. "No," I say quickly. "I got it. But thanks." The kitten holds my gaze as I step lightly toward it, trying not to sink deeper into the trash. It's quiet, watchful. "You're okay now," I say. "You're safe. I'm not going to let anything happen to you. I promise."

It's shivering when I scoop it up, runny yellow cheese stuck to its scrawny tail. Trembling and wet, its whole body fits right in the palm of my hand. I bring it close to get a better look and get a noseful of old Buddy's burgers and something else. Forest. Pine needles stick in his fur, like green stars in a night sky. But the kitten's eyes are bright and alert. "Hello there."

It regards me with curiosity, long black whiskers

twitching furiously. Emblazoned on its chest is a curious splotch of golden fur, like it's wearing a medallion. Or got hit by a paintball gun. "How did you get here?" I ask gently. "Are you lost? Did someone leave you? You must be super-strong to have survived that lightning bolt."

"Not superstrong. Not *possible*," Joe says. "Besides, she's not going to answer. Or he. Or whatever. Can you just get out of there already? Seriously. I'm going to barf."

Ignoring Joe's pleas, I flip the tiny kitten onto its back. "Boy," I declare. "I think so, anyway."

"Get out of there right now! I'm all the way stressed out!"

"Okay. Jeez. Relax." Cautiously, I retrace my steps, careful to keep the kitten balanced in my hand. I can feel his heart thumping strong and steady against my fingers. "Take him. I need both hands to climb out." I hold the kitten out to Joe, who recoils as if I am offering him a shopping bag full of vipers.

"I'm allergic," he whines. "And he smells. And he might have a disease. He shouldn't even be alive. He's probably a zombie cat. Or . . ."

"You're afraid of cats," I say flatly.

"I am not."

This animal barely weighs as much as an apple. Does Joe really think he's going to eat his brains?

"Fine." Gingerly, I tuck the kitten into the pocket of my hoodie, where he fits perfectly. "Don't worry, little guy. I'm getting us out of here, no thanks to Joe over there, who is afraid of you."

"No reason to be mean about it," Joe says with a sniff.

Back on solid ground, I pull the kitten out for closer inspection, only to find he is fast asleep.

Chapter 5

MINE

AS WE'RE WALKING HOME, Joe asks me every six seconds if the kitten is alive. He insists on double-checking that his tiny chest is rising and falling.

"He's sleeping," I say, annoyed.

"He might be dead."

"He's not dead."

"He's so small."

"Bacteria are small and they aren't dead. Why do you care, anyway, if you're afraid of him?"

"I'm *allergic*. And even if I wasn't, just because I'm afraid of something doesn't mean I want it to be dead. By the way, you smell bad."

I roll my eyes and increase my pace, frantically running through scenarios of what will happen when I get home wearing ruined shoes, smelling like a rotten corpse, and with a stray kitten tucked in my pocket. I'm almost certain Mom will be sleeping. But the remote possibility that she's not worries me. My jaw clenches. On the positive side, I have not given the other troubles in my life a single thought since getting struck by lightning.

Joe runs to catch up with me. "He needs a name. Can we check if he's alive again, please? Like, right now?" I give in to his pleading and pull the sleeping kitten from my pocket, but this time the black ball of fuzz opens one eye and scans us, as if taking our measure. "He's awake." Joe sounds so surprised, I realize he's not just being a pain in the neck. He really believes our small charge might be dead.

As I rub my knuckle gently between the kitten's velvety ears, I swear he sighs. "I'm going to call him Boots," I say.

"Huh? Why? He has, like, three white hairs on his back foot. You should call him Tuxedo. That golden fur on his chest looks like a bow tie."

"It doesn't look anything like a bow tie. It looks like the black hole photo. Hello, Boots." I bring the kitten up to eye level. Is he scowling? I think he's scowling. Okay, maybe Boots is a stupid name. Joe stands right next to me and peers at his face. The kitten yawns, showing off a set of tiny teeth.

"Fang?" Joe suggests.

"Are you kidding me?"

"Brainstorming here. Besides, *Boots*?"

"Okay. Not Boots. Not Tuxedo. Definitely not Fang. What about Forest? He smells piney, and he's got needles stuck to him like he just crawled out from under a tree."

"No way," Joe says, shaking his head. "You'd sound like a dork standing in the door and yelling 'Forest' when it was time for him to come in the house." He demonstrates, just so I'm clear. He might be right.

"So not Forest, either," I say. The kitten watches us as if he's a spectator at a tennis match: back and forth, now staring at Joe expectantly. "He's waiting. You better come up with something."

"Pumpkin?" Joe suggests. "Cuteness? Snowball? No. Wait. That only works for cats who look like snow. Never mind. Loki?" More yawning from the kitten. We're obviously boring him.

I nuzzle my nose into his fur. He does stink a little, but so do I. Joe paces around us, thinking. "Black Hole?" he suggests.

"Seriously?" I respond.

"You're right. No good. Gravitationally Completely Collapsed Object?"

"What does that even mean?"

"It's the scientific name for black holes."

"Oh."

"Thinking. Thinking. Okay. In 1905, Albert Einstein proposed the theory of relativity, which, among other things that I just don't have time to explain right now, predicted the existence of black holes."

Considering my recent fascination with black holes, this seems like something I should know. "He did? It did?"

"Yeah. So how about Albert? As a name, I mean." The kitten cocks his head and stares at Joe intensely. "Why is he looking at me like that?"

"Because he's plotting how to eat your brains." When Joe's eyes widen, I crack up. "He likes the name, that's why."

"He does?"

"Look at him." The kitten's miniature features are fully relaxed as he jams his head into my thumb, purring contentedly.

"He likes my name!" Joe dances a little jig on the sidewalk. "I have so many talents, I just didn't realize animal naming was among them. Hello there, Albert."

We keep walking. Albert's eyes drift closed. Being a kitten must be hard work.

"Are you going to keep him?" Joe asks. "Do you think maybe we should bring him to a shelter or something?"

My body reacts with a jolt. The thought of giving up my precious cargo turns my stomach. The minute our eyes met in the dumpster, I knew he was mine. "No *way*."

"But what if he belongs to someone?" Joe asks.

I stare at Joe, incredulous. I just pulled this barely born kitten from a dumpster. If we hadn't happened by when we did, he would have died. I shake my head. "Forget it. And even if he does have an owner, I would never give him back to someone so irresponsible."

"But maybe he just got lost?" Joe suggests

I level him with an unflinching glare. "Albert was abandoned, and he got hungry, and he crawled into that horrible dumpster, and he got stuck."

Joe looks down at his ruined shoes. "Okay. If you say so."

"I *do*," I reply, surprised at the intensity of my words. I'm the girl who is not brave enough to ask her best friend what is going on, but I have no such hesitation now. Albert belongs with *me*.

We arrive at the door to my house, a boxy two-story that looks particularly bleak in the gray afternoon. Dad liked to say that the house had "zero curb appeal," and that was why we could afford it. The neglected lawn has been overtaken by lanky weeds, and the raised flower beds where Dad lovingly tended vegetables and herbs are muddy and barren. My plan is to go into the house quietly and keep Albert under wraps. Being as my mother barely notices me, there's a decent chance he can live with us forever and she will never know.

A year ago I would have burst through the front door and presented Albert to my parents like a gift. I would have told them the unbelievable story of the storm and how I swear he called out to me in my head and how I rescued him. They would have listened intently, asking the right questions. We would have dashed right to the pet store for supplies, discussing the best cat food and treats and toys. We would have splurged on a really fancy cat tower so Albert would have something to scratch and so he'd feel welcome. At night they would have kissed me on the head, and then Albert, even if he smelled bad, while tucking us into bed.

We were a team. Mom was always the first one to the top of the mountain when we hiked. Dad carried the lunch. I brought the camera. Mom was fearless, and Dad was thoughtful, and I wanted to be a little bit like each of them. They said that no matter what happened, no matter how crazy life got, we would always have each other.

But those are just words.

After Dad died, it didn't take long for things to begin to unravel in a serious manner. Mom started having anxiety. Things like going back to teaching science at the high school or even to the grocery store paralyzed her with fear. The doctor gave her pills that she pops like M&M's, drifting around the house like a ghost, a willowy reflection of who she used to be. I try to put it out of my mind because if I think of it for too long, this giant lump forms in my throat and I can't breathe right.

At home I keep a low profile. In the beginning, whenever I entered a room, Mom would startle and look at me with a mix of fear and surprise. Going for invisibility seemed the best solution. I'm now an expert at making macaroni and cheese, buying groceries, and cleaning up the kitchen. I can do laundry, too, although last week a red sock got in with the whites and now my PE shirt is a weird shade of pink that is apparently permanent. But asking for a new T-shirt makes me feel bad. Lots of things make me feel bad, actually, and some days the noise in my head is so loud, I have a hard time concentrating. Today, however, those noisy spaces are filled with a steely determination that is unfamiliar but feels good. I don't *care* what Mom says. I'm keeping Albert.

"I gotta go," I tell Joe.

He grabs my arm, forehead creased with concern. "Will they let you keep him? Your parents, I mean."

"I'll figure it out," I reply.

"I'm worried."

"Don't be."

"Text me later."

"No."

"No? We just had a near-death experience together. Does that count for nothing?"

Great. Now he's mad. "I can't text you. I don't have a phone."

"No phone?" From the look on his face, you'd think this was the most shocking thing that happened all day. "How do you, you know, *function*?"

I could tell him about my dad and his idea that I participate in the actual world for a little longer, not just experience it through a tiny screen, and how that made me really angry at him and once I even told him I hated him for it. The memory swamps me with guilt. It's too much information. After all, Joe *remembers* things. "I just can't be bothered with one," I say, hoping he catches the whiff of haughtiness, like I am just so above the whole phone thing. But he just stares at me, bewildered.

"Wow. I always knew you were interesting, Cassie, but now I also find you a little confusing."

Joe thinks I'm interesting? I find that . . . interesting.

"I have to go," I say again. "Really."

"Okay. Good luck. You may have to feed Albert milk from a dropper. He's pretty tiny. I hope it works. Call me. Oh, wait. You can't call me. Maybe you can send smoke signals? I just live over there in the national park streets. You know, Yosemite. Yellowstone. Grand Canyon. I'm at 175 Acadia. I share a bedroom with Andrew, street side." I know his neighborhood. The houses on the national park streets do not lack curb appeal. "I guess I'll just hang by your locker in the morning, and you can give me an update?"

He's still chattering away about his bedroom and his brother and Albert as I shut the front door. And it occurs to me I have talked to Joe Robinson more in the last three hours than I have to any other person in months.

Chapter 6

HOME FREE. OR NOT.

THE ODDS OF WINNING THE LOTTERY are about one in fourteen million. The odds of my mother being at the kitchen table on the very day I want to sneak into the house undetected are one in one, because there she is. Her forehead rests on her arms, crossed on the table over a stack of unopened mail. She might be asleep. That would be excellent. Tiptoeing in these shoes is not going to be easy, but I'm willing to give it a go.

"You're home." Mom tilts her head up, eyelids half-mast. So much for tiptoeing. My fingers close gently around Albert, hidden from view. "How was your day?"

Well, I was struck by lightning, and I'm harboring

a contraband kitten in my pocket. "Fine. Nothing happened." Did I say that too quickly? Will she notice I'm acting weird? *Am* I acting weird?

Perking up, she sniffs the air. "Something smells terrible. Did you step in dog poop?"

No. That's my body after I rolled around in garbage. I shuffle my feet back and forth, hopeful she won't notice my ruined shoes. I don't have a good story for that yet either. I came in here like an amateur! What was I thinking? Miss Asher calls being organized "having your ducks in a row." If that's true, my ducks have gone berserk.

"And you're all wet." She eyes the puddle forming beneath me. Hoodie sweatshirts are not waterproof. They are, in fact, giant wearable sponges. Water drips from the bottom hem in a slow rhythm.

"It rained," I say flatly. I mean, everyone in Lewiston is always kind of wet. It's just how it is. In my pocket, Albert squirms. Time to end this conversation and get to the cover of my bedroom.

"I have a ton of homework," I say quickly. "There's a math test and a Spanish quiz, and I have to write an essay. So much homework!" I edge slowly out of the kitchen, careful to keep my hand in my pocket, lest my precious restless cargo decides to jump free right into Mom's lap.

"I was going to order a pizza for dinner," she says. Mom hasn't shown interest in dinner for months, so I should be ecstatic about the pizza, but mostly I just want to get away from her.

"Great! Love pizza. As you know." I'm definitely acting weird.

Just stop it right now, Cassie!

Mom glances at the mail fanned out across the table, bills and bank statements and junk. "I have to deal with these, I guess . . . ," she says, her voice trailing off. Her eyes take on that unfocused quality that is all too familiar. Normally, seeing it produces that giant lump in my throat, but today I'm on a mission to get to my bedroom, and there is just no time for lumpy throats. I take a step away. She shoves the mail into a haphazard pile. "Well, I can do it later. I might have a nap."

"Brilliant idea. You should do that."

I am almost home free. I have almost pulled this off. I imagine relaying the details to Joe in the morning. Wait. Why am I thinking about Joe? Never mind. Just keep moving down the hallway toward the stairs. Act normal. Relax.

Outside, there is a loud clap of thunder that throws me back on my heels. The sudden pounding rain on the roof sounds like a drum circle gone wild. The wind shrieks. It's like those weather gods suddenly flipped the switch back *on*.

"What the heck?" Mom startles, turning toward the window. In the driveway, a mini tornado has formed, sucking unraked leaves and chunks of dead weeds into its funnel.

An atmospheric event *twice* in one day? As Joe would say, *not* possible.

In my pocket there's a tiny sneeze, and a tendril of smoke rises into the air. This is followed by a muffled meow, and my dumpster refugee leaps from my pocket like his tail is on fire. Which it might be. A cloud hangs around him.

My mother, adrenaline already surging, leaps from her chair, scattering the mail all over the linoleum floor. "What is *that*?" she screams.

Is it normal for cats to spontaneously combust? It can't be, but still, Albert is somehow on fire. Well, smoking, anyway. Elbowing Mom out of the way, I rush to the kitchen sink, turn on the tap, and plunge him under the cold stream of water.

Cats and water? Yes. Trouble. Albert howls, a high, piercing sound that might rupture my eardrums. How can a creature this small produce a noise this big? My mother is yelling something in the background. Albert's needlelike claws dig into my flesh as he scrambles to get away. It had to be something from the dumpster stuck in his fur, something that ignited. Is old crusty ketchup a fire hazard? I can honestly say I have never thought about it before. This is just the sort of thing Joe could help me figure out. Ugh. Joe again.

Get it together, Cassie. This is a situation!

Mom leans on the kitchen doorjamb, rubbing the bridge of her nose with her fingers, a sure sign of exasperation. Outside, the storm dissipates, but she's forgotten about it already. "What is going on?" she demands.

I leave out the bit about the previous atmospheric event and Joe Robinson. Serving up an entirely plausible ketchup-as-combustible theory, I make sure to use fancy terms from our chemistry unit in science class. It sounds like I know what I'm talking about. I'm halfway to believing that cat fur plus dried sticky ketchup plus heat can cause a fire. But as I gently towel-dry Albert, Mom's face twists up, which means I know what she's going to say before she says it.

"Cassie, taking this on right now is too much." What she means is it is too much for *her*. "And that animal. It's so, I don't know, unhealthy-looking. Sickly."

I bristle at the suggestion. "He's just small," I say. "Not weak."

"So . . . fragile," Mom continues, as if she didn't hear

me, which she probably didn't. "I can't do this. I just can't. Not right now. It's too much."

I start to panic. "You won't have to do anything," I blurt. "I'll do all the work. I promise. You won't even know he is here. Please, Mom. I want to keep Albert."

"You *named* him already?" Mom looks aghast. She sinks back into her chair. There are heavy bags under her eyes. I don't mention that Joe actually named him, and I feel a little bit bad about taking credit for his work.

"I don't know if I can handle it," she says, almost to herself. "You know, with everything." She waves her hand around, vaguely referencing the "everything."

Last month I overheard a phone conversation between Mom and Aunt Julia. Aunt Julia must have suggested we relocate to Des Moines so Mom can heal and get her act together, but Mom freaked out, yelling about how she didn't want to move on, that she was terrified she'd forget his voice, his face. The rawness of her pain scared me, so I went to sit outside on the front steps until they hung up. But there is that steely sense again, deep inside me and louder than all the other noise. I'm *not* giving up my cat.

"I will do everything, I swear," I promise. Albert, having forgiven me for the impromptu dousing, snuggles into the towel, tucking his paws under his chest so he resembles a tiny bread loaf. I stroke his damp fur. "I'll feed him and clean the cat box and all of it. I swear you will barely see him."

Mom looks at me, really looks at me, for the first time in so long that I'm the one who startles. "You need this?" she asks.

There's weight to her question, the burden of conversations we haven't had because she can't manage them. I nod. "I do."

"Okay," she says with a sigh. "We can give it a try. But I promise nothing."

I squeeze her in a tight hug. "Thank you!"

"It's just a trial period," she says. But she hugs me back a little anyway.

Sitting on my bed, I gently lift Albert from the dish towel. He purrs and rumbles. I hold him up and stare into his eyes. He stares back, whiskers twitching, tail swishing.

"You have to be good," I say. "Like, perfect. We are on trial here."

Does Albert shrug, like "no big deal"? Can cats do that? Okay, it's time for me to acknowledge that I don't know much about cats or how to care for them. I know he has to eat and drink and poop and do all the things that living creatures do, but what else? How am I supposed to know what I don't know? Oh no. Was Joe right? Should we have turned Albert over to a shelter?

No. Don't think like that, Cassie. You got this!

The little fuzz ball is probably starving. I mean, he was trying to eat old Buddy's burgers from a dumpster when we found him, and seeing as Buddy's burgers aren't the best when they are fresh, that's all sorts of desperate.

"Let's start with dinner," I suggest. Albert cocks his head to the left like he is listening for what comes next. "Do you like tuna? You know, fish? Or maybe milk? Yogurt? Cheese? Ham sandwiches?"

Oh boy. Albert wrestles free of my grip and lands softly on the worn carpet. He hunkers down low, and his pupils expand with pure determination. His furry butt wiggles.

"What are you doing?" I ask. "We were talking about dinner."

"Grrrrr."

"Huh?" Suddenly Albert launches himself at something on the carpet. A spider! I leap to my feet. "Don't eat that! Gross! What if it's poisonous?"

But when I attempt to free the spider, Albert bats me away with a tiny paw. Jeez. Doesn't he know spiders eat mosquitoes, the world's most dangerous animal? I guess not, because he munches away deliberately on his leggy victim, ignoring me completely.

When Albert is done snacking on the spider, he jumps up on my bed and curls into a tight ball right in the center of my pillow, his tail draped over his nose. "Make yourself at home, why don't you?" I ask.

"Mew," he replies, a sound so small it's easy to miss.

"Mew yourself," I say. But just seeing him there on my pillow sparks a flicker of joy in my chest. I lie down beside him, watching him inhale and exhale. He sighs contentedly.

And I swear I get a heady whiff of singed plastic.

Chapter 7

MORNINGS ARE FOR SUCKERS

IT MUST BE RAINING AGAIN. And there must be a hole in the roof that is leaking, because the drops of water are hitting my face in exactly the rhythm of rain. Great. Raining outside. Raining inside. Where does a girl have to go to get away from the rain? I should really wake up and get a bucket or a towel or . . . wait a minute. Rain isn't sharp.

Swimming up through sleep, I open an eye to find Albert sitting right beneath my chin, tap-tapping my cheek with a soft paw. I guess he's been at it for long enough with no success that he has added one needlelike claw for emphasis.

Wake up! Feed me! I swear he grins.

"Albie," I mutter. "You are a cutie, the cutest ever, but

please can I have five more minutes?" He adds another claw to let me know the answer to my question is no. But I'm tired. Positive I was going to roll over and crush him, I kept waking up in the night, checking to make sure he was still breathing and cursing Joe for making me paranoid. My eyes are crusty, and my brain is full of fog.

Tap. Tap. Tap. Ouch!

"Fine. I'm up. Stop that. I get the point." I bury my face in the pillow for one more second, and when I do, I feel something scratchy and sharp. It's a burn hole in the pillowcase about the size of a dime, as if someone dropped a lit match on the fabric. The black jagged edges of the hole disintegrate when I stick my finger through. Perched right beside my head, Albert watches me with curiosity, whiskers twitching.

"Probably just the washing machine on the fritz," I explain. That seems reasonable, doesn't it? Albert cocks his head. I'm about to ask him what he thinks when I glance at the clock, which jolts me fully awake.

School!

Too distracted last night to remember to turn on my alarm, I'm now *late*. Usually I try to be quiet in the morning so as not to wake up Mom, but this is mission critical. Yanking open my dresser drawer, I berate myself for messing up the trial period *already*. A call from school will be bad. And no clean underwear. Great. When was the last time I did laundry? Judging from the Everest-sized pile heaped in the corner, I'd guess a while. I sift through the dirty clothes, frantically sniff-testing until I find a passable pair of leggings and a sort of clean hoodie.

Albert finds all of this terribly amusing, sitting on the bed tracking my panicky movements with his big green eyes. I can almost hear his critical assessment. *Slow down! You're just making everything worse!* But maybe that's giving him too much credit? Catching a glimpse of hoodie strings beneath a bunch of dirty socks, he leaps into action.

And I do mean "leaps."

My bed is tucked in one corner of my room, and the laundry pile is clear on the far side, a diagonal distance of probably eight feet. Crouching low, Albert wiggles his tiny butt and launches himself into the air. For a second, time seems to lurch and slow as he sails through the air, much too high, eyes latched on his prize, paws out like Superman. And my brain says this is not possible. My brain says this kitten is defying some important law of physics that Joe would surely know.

Albert lands with a thud, submerged fully under the pile of laundry. A striped sock flies into the air. His straggly tail sticks straight up like a flagpole. I have to go to school. I have to be in my seat in Mrs. Yamamoto's math class in exactly twenty-three minutes. Considering it takes me twenty minutes to walk there, and I still have to feed Albert, I am cutting it close. But here I stand, gazing with awe at my mighty kitten, who gleefully mauls the sweatshirt. The flicker of joy in my chest from last night ignites and fills all my senses. I can't stop smiling. Scooping up my ball of fluff, I hold Albert to my face and breathe in his smell. He still smells like garbage and melted plastic and pine needles despite yesterday's impromptu dousing.

"Snuggle face," I say in all seriousness. "You need a bath." He glares at me, wiggling to break free. It's clear I interrupted something important. I now have twenty-two minutes to get to school. Oh boy. In a mad dash, I race to the kitchen, fill a bowl with leftover tuna fish, and race back to my room. "Listen up, kitty-kins," I say, out of breath. "Be good today. Don't, I don't know, eat anything you shouldn't or break anything important or bug Mom. Actually, don't go near Mom. Okay? Okay."

But still I linger. Albert has food and water and a litter box made out of a cardboard container and shredded newspaper. He will be fine until I get home from school. It's just, I don't want to leave him. Not even for a second.

Go to school, Cassie! Don't ruin everything!

Right. On it. I press my lips to the small space between Albert's ears and deposit him in front of the tuna. "I'm sorry," I explain, "but school is not optional. I'm leaving. I. Must. Go." But before he dives into his tuna, I catch a flash of something in his eyes. It's a look I've seen in my own eyes, when Dad was gone and suddenly nothing was familiar anymore.

Lost.

Albert looks lost.

I remember Joe suggesting just that and my insistence that Albert was abandoned. But what if Joe was right? What if Albert has a home and he wants to go back there? By the time I think I might have to ditch school to stay home and comfort my cat, the lost look is gone, and Albert is back to devouring his breakfast.

Well. Okay then. He is no longer the least bit bothered by my quick exit.

Miss Asher says cats are above the fray. They love you on their own terms. They are not needy or desperate. They don't beg and plead for attention. But when a cat sits on your lap and stares into your eyes, you feel they are looking deep inside your soul. They *know* you. Now, I don't know about any of that, as I have limited experience being a cat owner. Fewer than twenty-four hours, really. All I know for sure is Albert likes stinky laundry.

I fly through the doors of Washington Middle School, just as the first bell rings, which is some kind of miracle because sprinting on my mangled shoes is no easy thing. I have not brushed my hair or my teeth, my socks don't match, and my hoodie is not as clean as I thought. A faint brownish stain is spread across the front. Maybe I can wear it inside out? Can I pull that off, or will I just look like the big dork Mia's friends already think I am? And what if the stain soaked through? Not good. But why am I thinking about this? I have two minutes to get my books and get to class.

I charge down the hallway to my locker only to find Joe pacing frantically in front of it, gnawing his fingernails with great determination. When he sees me, his face fills with a blend of anger and relief. I feel instantly guilty, although I'm not sure what I've done except show up late.

"*Where* were you?" Joe demands, throwing up his hands like an exasperated parent. "Is Albert alive? Can you keep him? Did you feed him? And I have something to show you! You really need a phone. I don't think I can live like this."

"I'm late!" I bleat. "Move!" I shove him aside and dig into my locker for my blue binder.

"There's really only a ten percent chance you'll get in trouble," Joe insists. "Tell me how Albert is."

"Albert is fine!"

"You're *sure*?"

"Yes," I say, panting. Sprinting can take a lot out of a girl who does not normally, you know, sprint. "He's fine. For real." A memory of the second storm and an image of the burn hole in my pillowcase and that lost look on his tiny kitten face, fleeting as it was, float in the periphery of my mind, but I swat them away. They don't mean anything. They *don't*. "I even made him a cat box out of cardboard. Can you get out of my way?" A 10 percent chance I'm going to get in trouble is still too high.

But Joe is not done yet. He pulls out his phone. "You need to watch this. But it's kind of . . . well . . . The guy . . . is . . ."

"Did you not hear the part about me being late?"

"It's important!"

"Oh, just give it to me, already." If I'm going to get to class only by watching this video, I better get on with it. But when the video starts, I jolt to full attention. "It's the vampire guy!"

"Huh?"

"From the library. He was arguing with Miss Asher yesterday. Sheldon something? She said he had mixed up his means and his ends, whatever that means."

"Sheldon Slack is his name. Why do you call him a vampire?" Joe asks sincerely.

I stare at him. "You don't see it?"

"See *what*? I don't know why you are obsessing about vampires all of a sudden, but *listen*. He's talking about the storm. *Our* storm."

"I'm not . . . never mind." I turn up the volume. On screen, Slack wears a white button-down shirt, sleeves rolled to the elbows. The puffy orange jacket is draped over the back of the chair. In the shadowy lighting of what must be his kitchen, he looks even *more* vampire-y. How does Joe *not* see it?

"I've been studying extreme weather for a decade," Slack says. "I'm the youngest professor of atmospheric sciences in the history of Lewiston University. That means I'm really good at my job. Like, the *best*."

I hit pause. "Why am I watching this, again?"

Joe sighs, exasperated, and taps the play button so the video resumes. "Just *watch*."

Slack fidgets. He drums his fingers on the wooden dining table, stacked high with cardboard boxes labeled *Research #1*, *Research #2*, and so on. I wonder if this is the research into a clue or an answer that Miss Asher referred to that is keeping him from visiting his parents. "I feel like that is reason enough for people to listen to me. What we witnessed last night, right here in Lewiston, the severe sudden onset of traumatic weather, is what I've been saying happens all along. The storms come first, followed by a dragon."

I hit pause again and eyeball Joe. "*A dragon?*"

"If you don't be quiet and just watch, I'm going to scream," Joe responds. Something in his face makes me believe him. The last thing I need is a scene in the hallway.

"Okay! Fine. Watching."

In the video, Slack rubs his eyes. He looks exhausted, clearly a man who has gone days without sleep. His hair fringe sticks out like he's been standing in the path of one of his extreme weather events, perhaps even a hurricane. "If my extensive research is correct—and why wouldn't it be, because honestly, I am very smart—this storm indicates that a dragon entered our dimension yesterday. My friends, I *must* find this dragon. It is critical. I cannot save humanity from pain and suffering if I don't. And I truly believe that is the reason I exist. To do *this*. Now, I have tried the regular channels. The FBI has a division. Their job is to sort out stories that seem impossible. Surprised?

Of course you are! We live in a world where we believe any-one can know anything. Nothing can be unknown. But you are very wrong."

He pauses, wiping a sheen of sweat from his forehead. He clears his throat. On the bottom of the screen, a phone number flashes, as well as an email address. "There will be a substantial reward for information that leads me to this dragon. As in a *lot* of money." He grimaces at the camera as if the idea of a reward is distasteful. "I *will* find him. I *have* to find him." Miss Asher called Sheldon Slack obsessed, and from his frantic, pivoting eyes, I'd say she is spot on. A bell rings, but I've forgotten about being late for class. There is something about Slack that makes it hard to look away. His desperation feels physical, as if I could hold it in my hand. I frown at Joe.

"Where did you find this?" I ask.

"Storm research," Joe replies. "He was basically the only one on the entire internet to mention our storm, which is kind of strange, don't you think? I mean, a kid farts in class and the whole world is making fun of him within twenty-four hours, so what are the chances that a significant weather event like ours just doesn't get talked about? It's weird. That hail was no joke! But I searched all the national weather data, and there was nothing reported. It was like the storm never happened, except we know it did, you know? But more importantly, what do you think about his *dragon* theory? I will admit that caught me by surprise."

My mouth has gone dry, and I feel unsettled, twitchy. I think his dragon theory means he's not okay, that something in his brain is wired wrong. He's scrambled, just like Miss Asher said. "Can we talk about this later? I have to go to class, and, actually, so do you."

Joe shrugs. "Dragons and weird weather are much more interesting than PE."

A few stragglers loiter in the hallways, kids who don't care about missing class. But I'm never late. *Never.* And I won't start now.

"I have to go," I say through gritted teeth. I owe Joe nothing. We are not friends. Just because he happened to be with me when I discovered Albert in the dumpster does not mean a thing.

"Fine. Go. Whatever. We will talk at lunch. Meet me in the cafeteria."

"Okay!" I bark. "Going!"

Only halfway through math class do I realize I agreed to have lunch with Joe Robinson and what that actually *means.*

Chapter 8

DO I REALLY WANT
WHAT I THINK I WANT?

THE WASHINGTON MIDDLE SCHOOL cafeteria is where dreams go to die. No, I'm not being dramatic: a girl can walk in popular and walk out invisible. Or worse, humiliated. Long tables line the space like horizontal stripes, and from the wide entrance, I quickly find Mia and her new friends on the far side of the room. Can I sit with them? Am I allowed? Or invited? Or whatever it is? Will sitting with them be worse than not sitting with them? Heat rises in my cheeks. I never should have shown up here without a plan. But I was so distracted by Albert and being late, I just didn't think about it. Albert. How cool it would be to just be home sitting on my floor, playing with him. I wonder what he's doing. I hope he's not causing trouble.

Cassie! You have a situation! Pay attention!

Right. Frozen in place, I scan for other options and rapidly realize there are none. I don't have any other friends. Either I sit alone or I make a foray into the land of Mia and friends. I wipe my sweaty palms on my shorts, all interest in actually eating lunch gone. Will anyone notice if I just slink away to the school library? Mr. Lee is usually willing to let me hide out there if I'm quiet and reading.

But now it's too late. Nestled within her protective posse of pretty girls, Mia sees me. Does her hand move to wave me over just from muscle memory? I can't tell. We stare at each other for a flash. It might be an invitation to come sit down. Is it? Are we suddenly good? I take a step toward them, but Mia quickly averts her eyes. A flood of nausea rises up from my stomach, and I'm keenly aware of the stain on my hoodie and my unbrushed hair. My cheeks burn and sweat dampens my forehead and tears prick the corners of my eyes. What did I expect? I heard what they said about me. I know how they feel.

Just turn around, Cassie. Just leave.

But then Joe Robinson, tucked in an empty space

between two groups of friends, gets up from his seat and waves frantically.

"Cassie! Over here." Does the whole Washington Middle School cafeteria fall into silence? Why yes, I think it does. Fortunately, my cheeks are as red as humanly possible already. There is no more redness to be had. "I saved you a seat." Everyone stares. People who did not know I exist suddenly are aware of me, and not for any reasons I want.

"He has *lots* of seats," a boy mutters. "Who wants to go near him?"

"Hide your phone," another adds.

Still stuck fast, unable to move my feet, I watch Joe's face almost as if in slow motion. His happiness at seeing me, at having a plan for lunch, for potential company, evaporates at my hesitation. Mia and her friends giggle. Don't they? I swear I can hear them.

But just yesterday, Joe offered to climb into that terrible filthy dumpster with me. He said he would help me if he had to. And just like that, my feet start to move forward. As I snake through the tables, the staring eyes begin to fall away. My fifteen seconds of infamy are over.

"Hi." I slide into the vacant seat across from Joe. On his tray is today's hot lunch, a sad thin turkey burger, a bunch of grapes, and a container of milk. He has not taken a single bite.

"Hi," he replies. It comes out sounding like an exhale, like he was holding his breath. He leans in. "How is Albert? I want all the details."

"There's not much to tell."

"Will your parents let you keep him?"

This is the perfect chance to tell him the truth about my dad, about my family. But this whole cafeteria experience has left me exhausted. "Yeah," I say. "They are cool with it."

Joe looks wistful. "You're lucky. My mom says no animals. She says she has enough to deal with already. She means me and my brothers."

"I got that."

"Okay. Sorry. Anyway, no pets. I'd like a dog. You know, someone who would listen to me without interrupting. It's hard to say anything in my house without someone shouting over you. Like, just try to get someone to pass the butter at dinner." He rolls his eyes, poking at the anemic turkey burger, which is almost guaranteed to taste like cardboard. The cafeteria does a decent macaroni and cheese, but beyond that they are culinarily challenged. I'm thinking about this when I notice Joe is drumming his fingers and anxiously watching my face.

"Are you getting lunch?" he asks.

"Maybe. It looks gross."

"It's always one hundred percent gross," he says. "That's not news. But I will wait for you if you want." And it occurs to me that Joe is lonely. Me sitting here with him—*me*—must feel like hope. "I want to talk about this Sheldon Slack guy. He says there are going to be more storms. What do you think?"

I have not been asked what I think about anything in a long time. "Maybe they have peanut butter and jelly," I say, standing. "I'll be right back."

Joe beams. "Great. I'll be here. Right here. Waiting. No problem."

Has anyone ever been so happy to hang out with me? If Mia was, it was so long ago, it doesn't count. Dad liked to hang out with me, but I don't want to think about that.

I grab a tray and load it up with a sandwich, milk, and a small plate of green grapes. It's hard to mess up grapes, right? It's not like the cafeteria has to do anything other than wash them. As I'm contemplating whether I can get away with a bag of chips, I get a big whiff of cheap flowers, a sweet cloying scent that knocks me back on my heels. Mia.

Last year we spent two hours in Nordstrom sniffing so many perfumes, I thought I might puke. She kept asking me what I thought of the different scents, but when I told her, she never liked my answer, so finally I just asked her what she thought and agreed with whatever that was. Too strong. Too peppery. Too citrusy. Whatever. I could not believe she thought perfume shopping was fun.

"It's important," she told me in all seriousness. "A girl needs a signature scent. It has to be perfect."

Finally she settled on Flower Me! and the next day when we met to walk to school, I could smell her coming two blocks away. I did not mention that I thought you were only supposed to use a little bit, not bathe in it. She would not have welcomed my opinion.

My stomach clenches instantly. I ignore her, pretending she's not standing right beside me. She pokes me in the shoulder.

"What is *wrong* with you?" she hisses. Other than I'm the opposite of fun? And all my clothes come from Target? But I don't say that. I don't say anything. I try to smile, but my face feels strangely beyond the control of my brain. "Joe Robinson is bad. Like, really bad. You *know* what he did to me and yet you *sit* with him? I mean, seriously, Cassie. Like, for real." Her hands are on her hips. Her lower lip juts out in emphasis. Her pretty, perfect posse watch from their perch.

I want to vanish. I want to scream. I want to shove her. But I don't do any of those things. Instead I mutter something about not seeing them at their table and Joe and I having a science project that is due. The words flow out of me like a river of nonsense. My hands shake, rattling the lunch tray with such force that I almost send the contents flying into the air. I wish Albert were here. I wish I could put my hand on his furry body.

"Whatever," Mia says, interrupting me and rolling her eyes. "You better come and sit with us before you, like, *ruin* me forever."

Hopefulness surges in my chest. Mia *does* want me to sit with her new friends! I knew she'd come around! Dutifully, I follow her to her table, watching her sleek hair swing like a horse's tail.

Out of the corner of my eye, I see Joe Robinson, staring down at his lunch tray, lips drawn into a tight thin line, and the hopefulness in my chest collapses into something that feels like shame.

Chapter 9

SOMETHING IS HAPPENING IN LEWISTON

SITTING WITH MIA AT LUNCH, I was too nervous to eat. The other girls ignored me. Mia ignored me. But I was there, wasn't I? I was back in the fold. I look for Mia after school, secretly hoping she will be waiting to walk home together, like we used to, but she is nowhere to be seen.

As I walk to the library alone, I try to keep the look on Joe's face out of my head. When I think about it, it leaves me a little winded, like I just did a bunch of sprints in PE class. I don't know why. We aren't friends or anything. We shared one weird experience together, but so what? It doesn't mean anything. Mia and I have been best friends since kindergarten, and that's a *long* time. But trying not to see Joe's face in my head is turning out to be harder than it should be. It keeps popping up anyway, uninvited.

Outside City Hall, between school and the library, a small crowd of maybe twenty people has gathered around a television-news van. A reporter, long dark hair perfectly coifed and wearing a suit that is totally inappropriate for our weather, holds a microphone to her red-lipped mouth. Because nothing ever happens in Lewiston, I slow down to see if something might *actually* be happening in Lewiston.

"Two odd and unexpected storms occurred in this quiet seaside college town in the last twenty-four hours," she says into her microphone. "Their unusual nature has experts scrambling for answers." I edge closer. "I have Maria Diaz, mayor of Lewiston, here. Mayor Diaz, what are your thoughts on these powerful, abrupt storms?"

This is the same mayor who visited our middle school last year. She has a big, loud laugh that made me want to laugh along with her even if I had no idea what was so funny. But she is not laughing now.

"These storms were severe in nature and really came out of nowhere," Mayor Diaz says. "We have a tsunami warning system in place, and one for fire, but we had no notice of these weather events until they were upon us. Fortunately, no one was injured, but they caused a lot of property damage in a very short time. One of our beloved coastal live oak trees, in Community Park, was struck by lightning. We don't know if it is going to survive." She sounds close to tears. A hush falls over the scattering of people. I guess Joe was wrong about the storm going unnoticed. The mayor sure seems broken up over it.

"Thank you, Mayor," the reporter says. "And now back to the studio."

"Wait!" There's a disturbance in the small crowd as a man pushes close to the front. He wears a baseball cap, so I don't immediately recognize his face, but there is no mistaking that puffy orange jacket. My mouth drops open. Sheldon Slack *again*? I feel like I'm being haunted. Why is this guy suddenly everywhere?

"Mayor Diaz! A question!" The mayor, just seconds from escaping back into City Hall, pauses, regarding him warily. I can tell from her expression that she knows him and is not exactly pleased.

"Professor Slack," she says evenly. "Now is not the time."

"Has anyone from the federal government contacted you?" he asks. "Do they plan to investigate?"

"The federal government is not interested in our weather hiccup," she says.

"But the Project Analog agents work on just this sort of phenomena!" Slack insists. "They will want to know what happened here."

"I think you spent too much time on the internet, Professor," the mayor says. "I don't know what you are talking about." But there is a flash in Mayor Diaz's eyes that makes me think she *does* know exactly what Slack is talking about, even if the rest of us have no idea. While some of the crowd drifted away as soon as the news team packed up their gear, a few remain, watching this exchange between Mayor Diaz and Slack. Including me.

"They are part of the United States Federal Bureau of Investigations," Slack says evenly. "They are a real thing. They investigate phenomena that are...otherworldly. Para-normal. Different."

Mayor Diaz rolls her eyes. Uh-oh. "Professor," she says. "While I am truly sorry for the loss of your brother when you were young, your ideas about what might have saved him are not . . . sound. And I simply don't have the time to indulge in childish fantasies. There is work to be done for the city of Lewiston."

"But . . ."

Mayor Diaz holds up her hand, cutting him off. "We're done here. You have a nice day, Professor."

Sheldon Slack's shoulders slump in defeat. He pulls off his baseball hat and wraps a bit of hair around his pointer finger, twisting it hard. Under his orange jacket, his shirt is rumpled like he slept in it. He does not notice the handful of people staring at him. He just walks away, muttering to himself and twirling his hair fringe, and I find myself trying to sort through what I just heard. Slack's brother? Project what? The FBI? But nothing ever happens in Lewiston! Certainly not at an FBI-level of interest!

As I'm mulling over current events, I notice two women wearing dull black suits and white shirts. I only notice them because of the sunglasses. No one wears sunglasses in Lewiston, on account of there being no sun here. A dead giveaway that you are from somewhere else is a pair of sunglasses. Shiny badges are clipped to their waistbands. I'm too far away to see what they say, but it's a safe bet they are not Lewiston police. They seem much too together for that. Are *they* FBI? The Project whatever that Slack was going on about? FBI agents always wear boring suits and sunglasses on television. Or maybe they are here asking questions about who hacked NASA? Why didn't I think of *that*? Oh boy.

They follow Slack from a discreet distance. He's so busy playing with his hair, he does not notice. And before

I realize it, I'm following *them* following *Slack*. One of the women is short with red hair and invisible eyebrows. The other has gray hair cut in a sleek bob. Who are they? Why doesn't Slack turn around? Are they here to arrest me and Joe?

I'm lost in these thoughts when I bump smack into Mia and the girls. I can't believe I have the nerve to call *Slack* clueless. My first instinct is to run, like I have inadvertently crossed paths with an apex predator—a tiger or a polar bear. But being as Mia already sees me, running would be weird. Instead I make like a frozen Popsicle with a dopey smile plastered onto my face, Sheldon Slack, Mayor Diaz, and the mystery suit ladies all but forgotten. Sure, Mia didn't wait for me after school, but we *did* eat lunch together, right? I didn't imagine that part.

Mia walks up to me, girls trailing behind in a V formation, like a flock of geese. She dresses like them now, in torn jeans and Ugg boots, but real ones, not the knockoffs. I wonder if her position in front means she has graduated to being their leader already.

"What's going on here?" she asks without even a hello, gesturing at the few lingering spectators.

"The mayor was talking to the news about the storms," I reply. "You know, the ones that happened yesterday."

"Why does everyone freak out over a little rain?" Mia asks, full of disgust, as if interest in the recent weather is some kind of personal affront. We used to joke about how nothing ever happens here in Lewiston, but now that something might be, even if it is something as boring as the weather, Mia is annoyed. It's as if being interested or at least curious is somehow weak or wrong.

"I don't know," I say too quickly, trying to match her tone of disinterest.

"Adults are so *not* okay," Mia says. The girls murmur their agreement. I have no idea what to say or do next, so I just stand there like a signpost, waiting.

"I'm having a sleepover," Mia says, finally breaking the awkward silence. "Friday night. Are you in?" Her gaze is steady and distinctly cold. But I know she can be like that. Besides, she is inviting me to a *sleepover*! It has literally been months and months since I've slept over at Mia's house.

"Yes!" I bleat.

Jeez, Cassie, way to sound desperate.

But I don't care. The other girls scowl as if they are not happy with this turn of events. But I'm not sure they ever smile, so I decide not to dwell on that.

"Maybe wear a hoodie without a stain?" Mia says pointedly. Ugh. I really should have turned this one inside out and hoped for the best.

"Sure," I reply brightly. Now what? Maybe they'll invite me to come with them to the coffee shop. Or to hang out in the park. I'm supposed to do my volunteer hours at the library, but if they ask me to go with them, I will just make some excuse to Miss Asher. She will understand.

But they don't ask me to join them. No coffee shop. No park.

"I guess I will see you Friday," Mia says with a dismissive wave. She doesn't sound happy about it, but I might be overthinking the whole thing. She invited me. That's the part that matters. The V formation turns and drifts back down the sidewalk. I'm headed in the same direction, but I don't want to tag along behind them uninvited, so I just stay still, with the vague sense that I shouldn't have to work so hard to interpret every little move, gesture, thought, or word of someone who is supposed to be my friend.

But I head toward the library with a bounce in my step. Sure, there were some bumps in the road, but that happens in friendships, right? Not everything is smooth sailing. Sometimes you get on each other's nerves. That is totally normal. Isn't it? Right? Besides, I'm going to the sleepover!

Everything is just fine.

Chapter 10

AIR ALBERT

I FLOAT INTO THE LIBRARY, buoyed by the idea that Mia and I are friends again, to find Miss Asher behind her giant reference desk, wearing a magenta sweater that is so bright, it makes me squint. She's lost in thought and doesn't even glance up when I enter, which is odd because she is the kind of person who is fully aware if a patron sneezes all the way on the other side of the library while perusing a biography of Barack Obama. If a mouse even thinks about making a home in a dark corner, she knows. If someone leaves a candy wrapper on one of the tables in the teen section, she's on it.

"*If* it's true," she mutters to herself, "and that is a big if, *how* do I find the rips Edward wrote about? And then what happens?"

What? Who's Edward? Another friend who is not a friend, like Slack? Does she have a lot of those? In truth, outside of the library I don't know that much about Miss Asher. Or maybe she's tired. Maybe she needs more coffee. Adults always say that when they are spaced out. But I notice she taps the pale yellow notebook, the same one from the locked drawer with the brightly colored symbol adorning its cover. What is it about this notebook that puts her in a trance?

"Hi," I say a bit too loudly, betting she squirrels the notebook away in a flash. Yup. There it goes. Back in the drawer. Drawer locked. Awkward smile. Again I have the sense of catching her in the act. But of what? Reading? Writing? Doodling? "Is Joe coming today?"

I didn't intend to ask, but I want to tell him about Slack talking to the mayor about Project Analog and how she was not happy about it, and what does it all *mean*? Joe's face in the cafeteria, though—that's why he is not here. Something shifts way down deep in my belly.

Miss Asher glances at her watch. "Wow. Look at the time. Joe's supposed to be here now. Usually he's pretty good at letting me know when he's not going to make it. Maybe something came up."

Yes. He 100 percent hates me. That's what came up. "I'll get started putting those books away," I say quietly, the ebullience I felt from Mia's invite gone.

This must show on my face, a sudden deflation like the air just went out of my balloon. "Are you okay, Cassie?" Miss Asher asks, coming out from behind her desk. She takes me gently by the shoulders and looks directly into my eyes. "I'm always here to listen. Anything you want to tell me, it's cool."

I *want* to tell her everything, about Albert, about Mia, about Joe, but the words stick fast in my throat. I don't know how to explain the dense stuff swirling in my chest, and even if I did, I might not be able to say it out loud. I'm not good at that part. Instead I just smile and ask her what she thinks about the storms. Clearly *something* if she was muttering about it.

Her gaze drifts to the locked drawer, but she quickly pulls herself back. "The storms are unusual," she says finally. "And I don't fully understand them. There are things that are . . . confusing."

Are we still talking about the weather? Because it sounds like she has moved on to another topic. I take hold of a trolley of books waiting to be shelved. "I'll go get started," I say.

"What?"

"The books?" I respond.

"Right! Of course! Books!" Her smile is bright and completely fake. As soon as I'm a few feet away, she dives for that notebook.

I am having a very strange afternoon. It's just the sort of afternoon that Albert will want to hear all about. Well, actually, I don't know if he will want to hear about it, but I'm sure he'll listen anyway if I scratch him behind the ears while I talk. Or bring him treats.

I race to put away all the books and jog straight home, avoiding any further conversation with Miss Asher. That part is easy, as her head is bent over the notebook. I'll tell Albert about that part, too. Maybe he has an opinion about what is on those pages. For the first time in a long time I'm excited to go home.

I pick up my pace. I've been waiting all day to squeeze Albert's cute little furry body and inhale his woodsy, dish-soapy, garbage-y smell. When I think about Mia and Joe, I feel unsettled. When I think about Albert, my heart calms down to a normal rhythm.

Arriving at my house, I avoid looking at the flower

beds. Dad loved to garden, which might be the most boring thing in the entire universe. All that digging and weeding just to get, like, one lousy tomato that the rats eat before you can even pick it off the vine? No thank you.

But after he was gone, I tended his precious garden every day. I weeded and fertilized the basil and oregano and chives and sage. I trimmed the wilted stems off the rosemary bush and wrapped the lemon tree in an old sheet when the temperatures threatened frost. I even pruned the peach tree. Unfortunately, it looked like topiary done while blindfolded. I'm no artist.

But the garden flourished. New sprouts and shoots popped up from the soil, straining toward the miserly Lewiston sun. The garden should have made me feel good, connected to my father, but I was fixated on the stupid rosemary bush. It was so *happy*, bursting with new life, so blooming and fragrant, as if it didn't even care *at all* that Dad was not around to see it.

That was it. I stopped removing the uninvited plants. I stopped tending the new bits of green. And now I avert my eyes from the weeds that have taken over. I push them away, just like the image of Joe Robinson's face, and pull open the front door. I'm anxious to see Albert and find out how his day went, although I'm not sure how exactly he will explain any of it to me. I wish he could talk. That would be the best.

The house is quiet, but this is not unusual. Mom used to greet me every day with three questions: What is something good that happened today? What is something you wish had gone differently? And what is one new thing you are curious about? Now Mom is rarely awake when I come home from school. Normally I head to the kitchen for a snack, and today I should be extra hungry, having missed lunch on account of being too freaked out to eat, but instead I dash up the stairs and right to my room. When I throw open the door, the smell of smoky old campfire hits me hard. There must be something rotten in the laundry pile. Did I leave a leftover hot dog on the floor or something?

"Albert! Where are you?" I glance around the room, noticing a few dark burned spots on the carpet and the closet door that were not there this morning.

Just dirt, Cassie. If you'd clean better, your room would not be such a mess.

Okay, but . . . wait a minute. "Albert?" My tiny kitten balances on the narrow top edge of my closet door, like the main attraction at the Cirque du Soleil, looking proud as can be. How the heck did he get up there? It would be the same as me jumping directly onto the roof of our house from the ground, like some sort of superhero. *Impossible.*

I swear Albert winks just before he launches himself, a furry black missile shooting across the room. He hits me dead center of my chest, falling directly into my cradled arms and pushing his tiny cold nose into my forehead. "That was dangerous!" I admonish. "How did you get up there, anyway?"

But Albert is not telling. He settles in, kneading my forearm with his sharp little claws, and starts to purr. Okay. Maybe this flying thing is something cats do. What do I know, anyway?

"Hello, little guy," I say, settling down on my bed. "Did you have an exciting day jumping on things? I got an A on my math test. Good, right? And it wasn't an easy one. Because sometimes they are. And then there was the lunch thing. Where do I even begin that story?" Usually after I start talking, I imagine what I sound like to whoever is listening, and it is *never* good. That's why I keep my mouth shut. But Albert gazes up at me with complete understanding. Maybe I don't sound like such a dope to him. I press on.

"So Joe wanted to have lunch with me." Does Albert perk up at Joe's name? Does he remember him? "And I said I'd see him in the cafeteria, but I never committed to sitting with him." But I *did* sit with him. And I told him

I'd get a peanut butter and jelly sandwich and come *back*. Oh boy. "Anyway, Mia, that's my best friend—I think? Or she used to be? Anyway, she invited me to sit with her and her new friends, and I really want them to like me, so I did, but then Joe got mad at me, and, well, we're not even friends! Which means, does he even have the right to be mad at me? I don't know! And then I ran into Mia outside City Hall, where I watched Miss Asher's friend-slash-not-friend, Sheldon Slack, get into it with the mayor over whether or not she believed Lewiston has a federal-level-of-interest weather situation. Way weird."

Albert grumbles. I guess he doesn't believe Sheldon Slack any more than Mayor Diaz did. "But wait, it gets better! Mia invited me to a sleepover! With the girls! But then Joe didn't come to do his volunteer hours, and I really wanted to tell him about Slack because of the video this morning. Wait, did I tell you about the video?"

I'm giving myself whiplash as the words pour out. I try to fill Albert in on the backstory, how uneasy it has been with Mia since she upgraded friends and how I long for her to choose me again, even if that longing makes me feel bad. And I tell him about Miss Asher and the library and Joe and the black hole and the humiliating moment in science class when I made the mistake of asking about them.

Albert is a very good listener. Oh, wait. He's *asleep*.

I settle him onto my pillow and creep down to the kitchen to get a snack. There are slim pickings, but it feels like a win to find a half-full bag of slightly stale potato chips behind a box of cereal. Salt and vinegar. Even better! I wonder if cats eat chips. Another thing I should find out. I know that if dogs eat grapes or chocolate, it makes them sick, and I don't want to slip anything to Albert that will hurt him. I should ask Joe.

Joe. He keeps popping into my head. I should have at least explained why I didn't come back to sit with him. Right? Shouldn't I have? Why is this so confusing? Probably because I'm starving and nothing makes sense.

I'm about to dig into the bag when the doorbell makes me jump two feet in the air and spill half the chips on the floor.

"Not okay!" I bark. Stale chips are one thing. Stale chips covered in dust bunnies are another. Besides, no one ever comes to our house. I rush to the living room windows, peering out to see who it is.

And there stands Joe Robinson.

Chapter 11

THE TRANSITIVE PROPERTY OF LOST THINGS

JOE RINGS AGAIN and my mother appears, bleary eyed, pulling on a bathrobe with frayed cuffs. "Who's here?" she asks anxiously. On the rare occasion someone comes to our house and rings the doorbell, Mom always reacts in the same way, like something big is happening and her stress meter is deep in the red. She told me once that every time she hears the doorbell, she thinks it might be Dad, here to tell us that it was all a big misunderstanding, that he is right as rain, just got lost or something. When I said that I thought if that were the case, he'd just use his key, she started crying, and I went outside to sit on the driveway.

"It's my friend," I reply. This should surprise her, as the

last friend who came here was Mia, and that was ages ago. I wait for her questions about who it is and how long have we been friends and all that mom stuff, but instead her shoulders slump and her face goes blank. She mutters something and drifts down the hallway back to her bedroom. This kind of moment usually causes that lumpy thing in my throat, but right now I'm too busy wondering what Joe is doing here. Do I let him in? Do I pretend I'm not here?

Fortunately, Joe has plans. As I stand stock-still behind the closed door, he yells, "Cassie! Let me in! I know you are standing right there! I want to see Albert, and by the transitive property of lost things found, he partially belongs to me." Huh? "Don't make me stand here and scream, because I totally will."

Right. That would be bad. I pull open the door, and in steps Joe. I'm surprised at the relief I feel that he is here. Maybe he doesn't hate me. Maybe I haven't spoiled everything. The first thing I should do is apologize for abandoning him in the cafeteria. I should just open my mouth and say I'm sorry, because I think I really am. But he doesn't give me much of an opening. He's here for the kitten.

"Where is Albert?" he demands, skinny arms crossed against his chest, prepared to do battle if necessary.

"In my room," I say.

"I want to see him," he says with a sniff. "I want to make sure he's okay."

"He's fine," I reply.

"I don't know that I trust you," Joe says. Okay. I deserve that.

"Come on," I say, gesturing for him to follow. "This way."

"Great," he replies. "And I'll take those." In a flash he snatches the potato chip bag from my hand. "Ugh. Stale."

"Well, give them back, then."

"No way."

Fine. I push open my door, making room so Joe can enter first. "Is something on fire?" he asks, sniffing the air.

"Well, actually . . ."

"It's kind of gross. Where is he?"

"Here, kitty-kins!" I call. "Come on, fuzzy face, dumpling, cutie pants, Mr. Adorableness."

Joe stares at me, aghast. "*What* did you call him?"

"Kitty-kins. Fuzzy face. Dumpling. Cutie pants. And Mr. Adorableness."

"Poor Albert," Joe moans. Followed by "Ouch!" Albert, stealthy under an overturned laundry basket, stretches out a paw and whacks Joe in the ankle. "Bad kitty!" As if to prove Joe's point, Albert squeezes from beneath the basket and launches himself at Joe's shoelaces. Joe starts jumping around as if he is being attacked by murder hornets or something. "Stop that, you furry menace!"

I descend into a fit of giggles. "He's barely five inches tall."

"He's shredding my shoelaces! I've already ruined one pair of shoes this week! Get him off me!" Albert clings to Joe's shoe like a burr to a wool sock. Miss Asher once told me that cats have a sixth sense about who doesn't like them. She said *that* is the person whose lap the cat will immediately try to occupy.

Before things get really out of hand, I untangle the kitten from Joe's shoes and clutch him to my chest. Not happy about giving up the shoelaces, he scrunches up his face and glowers.

And his eyes turn *bloodred*.

A jolt of electricity rushes through me. "Joe," I whisper. "Look."

Joe, fixing his shoelaces, waves me off. "Busy," he says.

"Joe," I repeat. "Albert's *eyes*."

Something in my tone gets Joe's attention. Beside me, he takes one look at Albert's eyes glowing like red marbles and leaps back as if scorched. "What the heck?"

Is it just a trick of the light? Could that be all? Albert's needlelike claws dig into my skin. I think he growls. Outside, the sky darkens. A slender funnel cloud forms over the street. Rain beats on the roof. The tiny twister picks up speed and expands. The tree across the street bends under the pressure.

"It's happening again," I whisper. Joe nods, focus fixed on the window. Albert's claws dig deeper. His red eyes flicker like flames.

"Albert!" I yell, startling the kitten and Joe. "Cut it out. Enough!" Albert gives me a terse little meow, shakes his head, and suddenly the glowing red eyes are back to mossy green. The twister evaporates, fading into small wisps of fog and clouds. The sky brightens. But the tree across the street has been stripped of all its remaining fall leaves.

I stroke Albert between the ears while Joe does his best impression of a boy who is about to hyperventilate. "Did you see that?" he gasps. Yes. I did. All of it. Although I kind of wish I hadn't. I stand across the room, clutching my cat and waiting for Joe to say something, because right now the noise in my head is pretty loud.

"This cat is at least ninety-eight percent weird," Joe says flatly.

"No, he's not," I shoot back.

"Did you somehow miss those glowing eyes?" Joe yells. "That is not normal. They were, like, ruby red and sparking!"

"They were *not* sparking!" Why was I even feeling bad

about not treating Joe like a friend should? We aren't friends! We don't agree on anything!

He scans my room, taking deep breaths, regrouping. "And he never should have survived the dumpster in the first place! And why does it smell like fire in here? Burned plastic or something. Like when we found him."

Albert buries his head in my armpit, the cat version of covering your ears, like he doesn't approve of the arguing. Okay. So maybe I am forced to admit he is a little weird. Joe picks up on my hesitation. He narrows his gaze. "What are you not telling me?"

"About that," I say. "Do you think cats can spontaneously combust?"

Joe runs a hand through his hair. "You had better explain," he says. And so I tell Joe how Albert was suddenly smoking yesterday when I brought him home, and how he was on top of my closet door, and I point out the weird burn marks that are now all over my room. "And you have already smelled the smell. And sometimes he looks at me as if he is just so lost, like desperately sad or something. I mean, what if he's sick or there is something wrong with him?" My heart constricts at the thought I might lose Albert, and suddenly I'm just this side of crying.

Pacing the small space of my room, plowing right

through the mountain of laundry, Joe pulls out his phone, thumbs flying. I half expect him to run right into the wall.

"Cats with glowing red eyes," he mutters. "Cats spontaneously combusting. Cats causing massive weather disruptions. Nope. Nothing. What? Oh, no way, he doesn't have *that*. Ugh. Gross. Forget it. The internet does not know what I'm talking about." He jams the phone back in his pocket and immediately starts running his hands over his hair again. Maybe this is what he does when he's thinking. Or his head is just itchy. I settle into my desk chair and wait patiently, a now-sleeping Albert nestled in my lap.

"Okay," Joe says finally. "I have a theory. Actually I have about five theories, but let's start with the first one, which is Albert escaped from a secret government lab that was experimenting on cats, trying to make them into weapons or something. The CIA did this thing once where they tried to turn a cat into a listening device. They called it Acoustic Kitty. I'm not even kidding. Anyway, Albert got away and hid out in the dumpster and the storm was a coincidence because, like, global warming and everything, but Albert survived because he's not normal." He looks at me expectantly. "What do you think?"

"*That's* your theory?" I reply.

"I give that one about a seventy percent chance of being right. My next one is probably closer to fifty percent. Want to hear it?"

"Can I say no?"

He ignores me. "Remember Superman and how he came from a disintegrating planet and his parents put him in an egg spaceship and sent him to Earth because he was going to die otherwise?"

"No. Not a fan."

"Whatever. Maybe Albert was sent here from another disintegrating planet and he has superpowers and we need to figure them out. The storms are related to accessing his superpowers." This is hopeless. We are doomed. "Fine. Maybe we should just take him to a veterinarian and ask if he is okay."

Veterinarians cost money, and I don't have any. The trial period would end abruptly if Mom suspected Albert was sick. And he doesn't *seem* sick. Other than the weird stuff, as Joe so graciously put it, he seems just fine, strong and healthy and hungry and all the things he's supposed to be.

"I don't think I can afford the vet," I say quietly.

Joe eyeballs the sleeping kitten. "Maybe we should ask

Miss Asher what she thinks. She knows everything." This is true. Miss Asher is the smartest person I know. And if she doesn't have an answer, she can for sure help us find one.

I can tell by Joe's expression that he has already made up his mind that Albert is either a secret government experiment gone awry or some tiny furry Superman, but his Miss Asher reasoning is sound. Plus, you can trust Miss Asher not to freak out if you tell her something strange. She's good that way. We agree to go to the library tomorrow immediately after school.

Joe sits on my grungy carpet and teases Albert with the bouncing reflection from his watch face while telling me some ridiculous story about how he intends to jump off the Golden Gate Bridge with a wingsuit, if only he can get someone to sell him one. And give him a lift to the bridge.

But even Joe's outrageous stories don't help me focus. Now that I am thinking there is something potentially wrong with Albert, I can't concentrate on anything. I even forget to mention seeing Slack earlier with the mayor. In that dumpster, I promised Albert that I would keep him safe no matter what. I'm determined to do just that. Whatever it takes, I will not let any harm come to him.

Chapter 12

SHELDON SLACK IS EVERYWHERE

THE NEXT DAY, I hang out in the school library during lunch period, pretending to be super absorbed in a new novel that Miss Asher gave me last week. I'm much too stressed out about Albert to go through another cafeteria rodeo like yesterday. I can't even find time to worry about Mia and her gang of terrifying gal pals and how I might screw up the sleepover, which feels a little bit like an audition. But I still leave Joe waiting outside school until I am sure Mia has gone and won't see me walking with him.

Joe kicks a pine cone up and down the sidewalk, shoulders hunched, hands deep in his pockets. His baseball cap is askew. When I realize he thinks I'm a no-show, feelings of guilt roil my stomach. I pick up my pace. "Hey, Joe!"

His eyes find me and he grins. "There you are."

"Sorry," I say. "My locker jammed."

But on some level I know that he knows I was waiting out Mia. Suddenly I have the urge to tell him that if I *did* have a time machine and could coast along on the timeless event horizon of a black hole, I would go back to yesterday, pick up my peanut butter and jelly sandwich, and sit with him. Right? Isn't that what I'd do, given a second chance?

"Whatever," Joe says, waving me off. "Has anything else strange happened with Albert? Since yesterday, I mean?"

"No." Well, actually, there was a moment when Albert was chasing his tail and moving so fast, like impossibly fast, that he actually *disappeared* into a continuous blur. A fur-blur? And when he stopped, he wasn't even panting. I, however, was breathless. I don't share this with Joe because I'm worried that one more piece of evidence supporting his theory that Albert is a covert CIA spy device or an alien superhero will push him over the edge.

The number of people outside of City Hall has grown since yesterday, to maybe thirty, and there is no news van in sight. What are they doing here? If Lewiston has a hot spot, which it doesn't, this is not it.

"Cassie, is that . . . ?" Joe points to a man clutching a stack of flyers and surrounded by a group of people.

The puffy orange jacket! Sheldon Slack! *Again!* The bags under his eyes could hold a month's worth of luggage. "He was here yesterday," I say, "arguing with the mayor."

Joe is aghast. "And you just kind of *forgot* to mention it to me?"

"Well," I say, in my own defense, "you were mad at me because of the whole, you know, cafeteria thing. And I'm sorry about that. I . . . I'm just sorry is all."

Wow. Apologizing really *can* make a person feel better. It is as if someone emptied a few bricks out of my backpack. But Joe is not impressed. "Yeah. Yeah. Fine. That's great and all, but you should have told me you saw him. I mean, what are the chances?"

"Pretty good," I reply. "I see him every time I turn around."

Joe, pushing through the crowd to get closer to Slack, ignores me. "What's he saying? Can you hear him?"

In the middle of the crowd, Slack hands out flyers, blocky black lettering on fluorescent yellow paper, and tells a story. I will give him credit: His audience, though small, is attentive. They hang on his every word.

"These mosaic storms," he explains, "are extreme microbursts with wind and hail and tornadoes and lightning. They come in clusters. They are highly irregular. The last one to occur here was thirteen years ago. Before that it was fifty years."

His face clouds, seemingly momentarily lost in memory. But the restlessness of the crowd brings him back. They want to know if his story has a point, or are they just standing here in the drizzle for nothing? Joe pushes closer and snags a flyer. I can't take my eyes off Slack.

"Quite by accident, my high school best friend and I stumbled upon some research that linked these mosaic storms to the appearance of . . . dragons."

He said dragons again! Just like in the video! What is going *on* here?

"There is a story," Slack continues. "Do you want to hear it?"

A murmur ripples through the crowd. I expect the onlookers to react indignantly. *Don't insult our intelligence with tales of dragons!* But they don't. Instead they wait silently for his story.

"Very well," he begins. "To start, we must go back in time to when Lewiston was just a bunch of shacks and the whiff of gold was in the air. Edward Tenbrook was twelve years old and dirt poor, part of a large family who had come west, desperate to change their circumstances."

Slack does not look like he is much of a storyteller, but no one moves. "However, things did not improve for Edward," he continues grimly. "In fact, they got worse. There was no food, no shelter, and no gold. The family had spent pennies they didn't have on gold-panning equipment and now found themselves in debt to some very bad men." Concern ripples through the crowd. None of us know what is going on, or who this Edward person is, but we are a little breathless anyway. "And then, almost overnight, things changed for the Tenbrooks. They started to peddle a health serum. They claimed their potion could cure disease. They claimed it could save your *life*. The desperate and powerful descended upon Lewiston, demanding the serum, willing to pay just about anything to get it. Soon the family was rich beyond their wildest dreams. Everything was on the right track." Slack pauses and scans the crowd, gathering his thoughts. "But just as quickly, their fortunes reversed. On December eighteenth, an epic storm occurred. Hail. Wind. Torrential rain. Lightning that shook the ground. And it ended with the town ablaze. The fire is said to have begun at the Tenbrooks' estate late at night. By morning the town was wiped clean off the map."

Slack stops and holds up his flyer. "That storm was caused by a dragon coming here, and the fire was that same vengeful dragon's act of fury." He shakes the piece of paper. "There is a dragon among us *now*, and I must find him. Please. I beg you for help."

His words hang there over us, like a hummingbird hovering midflight, seemingly still but really pulsing with energy.

"A *vengeful* dragon?" Joe whispers, eyes wide. "I wasn't really counting on vengeful dragons, you know?"

Me neither. I swipe the flyer from his hands. Slack is asking people to bring him any information that might lead to this dragon. There's a reward. It's big. People murmur to each other.

"Hashtag DragonHunters!" shouts a woman out of the blue.

"Save Lewiston!"

"Free the whales!" another person yells, and a group of spectators bursts into laughter.

Slack's face grows dark. "This is not a joke," he says through gritted teeth, but it is too late. The group is getting rowdy, laughing and joking, as if some great tension has been lifted. I mean, come on, *dragons*? The flyers drift to the ground like snow.

The crowd melts away. They have already forgotten Slack was even here to begin with.

As we walk to the library, Joe says, "I don't know if I believe Slack, but Slack sure does believe Slack." He's right. Slack's story of dragons is outrageous, but he seemed 100 percent confident in the truth of it. It's magical thinking, just like Mom wondering if it's Dad every time the door- bell rings.

"It's probably global warming, anyway," I say. "You know, causing the storms. When the ice caps melt, all sorts of bad stuff happens."

Joe nods. "Or it could be the current planetary align- ment. Every once in a while, the planets line up. It has to do something to the universe, right?"

That seems more likely than dragons. "Maybe."

"If I had a jet pack," Joe responds, "I could go right into the eye of the storm and see if there are any dragons in there."

"I thought you wanted a wingsuit."

"That is turning out to be hard to get," he replies with a sigh. "I'm changing direction to a jet pack."

"Those are only in the movies," I say.

"Nope," he responds. "There was a guy in one spotted by a pilot landing at San Francisco International. For real."

"So you're just going to ask to borrow it?" A breeze picks up. I swipe tangled hair from my eyes.

"I have to find him first," Joe replies, straightening his cap. "I'm working on the problem."

I stare at him.

"What?" he demands.

"I get that you want to whiz around the sky in a rocket suit," I say. "It would probably be super fun. But you do have to consider that death is a real possibility, especially if you go flying into a tornado. Plus, what if the guy says no?"

He thinks about this for a long moment. "You might be right," he says finally. "I might need a plan B. Pretty sure NASA has jet packs. Maybe I can hack them and get one routed to my house."

"Hacking *and* stealing?" I ask.

"No?"

"Probably not."

We turn down the broad tree-lined avenue where the library is located. "Thanks," Joe says suddenly.

"For what?" I ask.

"Only a true friend will tell you when your plans have

flaws," he replies. "Let's go!" We race down the sidewalk to the library entrance, where Joe lets the door slam in my face.

"Joe."

"Oops. Sorry. Hurry up!"

It's time to get some answers.

Chapter 13

MISS ASHER IS HIDING SOMETHING

WE ENTER THE LIBRARY to find Miss Asher behind her big fortress of a desk, chewing on the end of a pencil. She writes exclusively in purple ink and keeps the pencils just for gnawing. Her habit is made slightly less gross only by the fact that she is aware of how gross it is and tries not to chew pencils in front of innocent people. Her hair, usually thoughtfully spiky and colorful, is lopsided and deflated, and she still wears the magenta sweater from yesterday. Her desk is littered with bagel crumbs and half-full mugs of coffee. Did she stay here all night? Why would she do that? Her perfectly nice house is only about a fifteen-minute walk away.

Her face is buried in the small yellow notebook with

the bright symbol on the cover. The pages are full of her swirly writing, and her focus is intense, like the answers to the great questions of the universe are right there in front of her if only she could puzzle them out. I want to tell her not to bother. The universe doesn't care.

Totally distracted, she doesn't hear us come in. This is the *second* time this has happened. Take that with the sweater and *something* is up. When we say hello, she jumps five feet in the air, eyes wide, hand flying to her chest. "Kids! You almost gave me a heart attack!"

We apologize and promise not to startle her again. Oh, who am I kidding? We fall all over each other laughing. It takes a few moments and a hardcore glare from Miss Asher for us to knock it off.

"Sorry to be so distracted," she says, rearranging the mess on her desk. I catch a glimpse of a fluorescent yellow flyer just before she covers it. Slack's flyer? "I'm just thinking about this weather situation we are having. All very unusual. But wait a minute. What day is today? Are you adding an extra day to your volunteering? I'm so happy to see you are coming together now. It's always nice to have a friend to do things with." Very interesting. Miss Asher thinks we are friends. I think Joe thinks we are friends. So *are* we friends?

Never mind that, Cassie! Focus! You are not here to talk about the weather or friendships or anything else! This is about Albert. Your new kitten is weird.

Right. "I found a kitten," I say. "And I have some questions."

"Oh, Cassie, that is great." Miss Asher quietly tucks the notebook back into the drawer and locks it. "Good for you. A pet can be wonderful for dealing with grief. I want all the details. Is your mom okay with you having a cat?" Miss Asher keeps telling me that Mom will snap out of her daze, that she will get better and be herself again. She says Mom is strong and I just need to be patient. But Miss Asher remembers my mother from a long time ago, back when she was still my normal mom. Not as she is now.

"Yes," I say too quickly. Now Joe is looking at me too, and I squirm. Of course, he's wondering what my grief is all about. I haven't told him about my dad, and now I can't remember why. Fortunately, we are here to ask about Albert, and Joe is easily distracted. Pulling off his hat, he runs a hand over his head. This is what he does when he's concentrating. I know that now. So maybe we *are* friends.

Cassie! Quit it!

"The other day," Joe begins, jumping right in, "Cassie and me are walking home, you know, after the printer exploded. And after I showed her the black hole photograph."

"In a book!" I blurt, thinking about those possible FBI agents crawling all over Lewiston. "That's where we saw a black hole picture. It was a thing in science class." It was definitely *not* an illegal hack into a government agency.

Joe's eyebrows rise to his hairline as he realizes how close he came to stepping into a minefield. "Yes," he says. "Exactly what Cassie just said. A *book*."

"Okay," Miss Asher says, nodding, her face a picture of complete concentration. "A black hole. Go on."

"Anyway, we are walking home, taking a shortcut through the alley behind Buddy's Burgers," Joe continues, "when suddenly, kapow! Out of nowhere! Crazy storm!"

"The one with the giant hail," I add. "Huge hail."

"Humongous," Joe agrees. "Like tennis balls."

"Or baseballs."

"Hold on," Miss Asher interrupts. "Did you say you were *in* the first storm?"

She's upset. I sure hope Joe doesn't mention that we were hit by lightning. "Um . . . yes?" I reply.

"Of course, of course." She gnaws a pencil. "Go on. Tell me more."

"Okay," Joe says. "So right after the storm just, like,

vanishes, we find this kitten in a dumpster—the same dumpster that was hit by lightning not five minutes before!"

Miss Asher's eyes go wide. Jeez, Joe, you had to go and mention the lightning. "Lightning?"

"Yes," Joe says, waving off her concern, "but don't worry about it. We had on rubber-soled shoes, which will save your life about seventy-five percent of the time."

Wait just a minute. I did not know those odds, and when we are talking about survival, they aren't that great.

"Oh dear." Miss Asher's hand covers her mouth in shock, but Joe doesn't notice.

"After we heard the meow," he continues, "Cassie got in the dumpster. I know. Totally gross. But she did it and found the kitten and that's Albert. I named him. All me. He's jet black, even his whiskers, with a big golden splotch on his chest. Like he's wearing a pendant or something."

Miss Asher jumps in the air as if *she* just got hit by lightning. "Like a golden blaze?"

"Uh, yeah." Another sidelong glance from Joe. "I guess so. But that's not the problem."

"Problem?" Miss Asher whispers. "What sort of problem?"

"The kitten does some stuff," I interrupt. "And I don't know if it's regular for kittens or what."

"*We* don't know," Joe corrects. "Albert lives with Cassie, but he's part mine."

I turn to Joe. "He is?"

"Transitive property, Cassie," he replies smugly. We are bickering about ownership of Albert, which is why neither of us notices at first that Miss Asher has gone suspiciously quiet and is suddenly extra pale. Her hands tremble, but she quickly sits down and slides them under her thighs. It is unnerving how downright unnerved she appears.

"Miss Asher?" I ask. "Are you okay?"

"You don't look so good." Joe leans close, examining her face for clues. "Do you need Twizzlers?" There is a long moment where she simply does not answer, staring at a fixed space beyond us in such an intense way, I start to fidget. Did we somehow break Miss Asher by asking about kittens? Should we call for help?

Finally she shakes her head, as if getting rid of a troubling vision, and refocuses on us standing in front of her big desk, waiting. "Kids," Miss Asher says in a serious tone usually reserved for reprimanding people who use their books as coasters. "What are the strange behaviors?"

I run down the list, starting with the spontaneous combustion and ending with the sparking red eyes. This information does not seem to help Miss Asher's condition. "You say you found the kitten after the initial storm?" she asks. "He is black and golden? Are you positive? As in absolutely and completely?"

I glance at Joe. Has the entire city of Lewiston gone loopy?

"Are we in trouble?" Joe whispers.

"No," Miss Asher answers quickly, "of course not. It's just . . . well . . . this information is very interesting. And I want to make sure I get it straight. Has anyone else seen Albert's unusual . . . behaviors? Does anyone else know you have him?"

"We haven't told anyone about Albert," I say.

Joe shrugs. "Who would we tell?" But the more important question is: Why does it matter? Miss Asher starts to pace, muttering and chewing her pencil so fast, she reminds me of a beaver.

"Are you sure you're okay?" I ask.

"What?" She stops, startled. "Me? Yes. Fine. Perfect. I have to check something. I thought only metallic . . . I'm having a thought is all." With that, she yanks the key over her head, opens the candy drawer, grabs the notebook, and darts into the privacy of her tiny office in the back, where she never, ever goes because she likes to be out among the patrons. But now she can't get there fast enough. She disappears inside and slams the door abruptly.

"What the heck just happened?" Joe asks, staring at the space that used to hold Miss Asher.

"I don't know," I reply with a shrug. I can't even guess.

And we don't get a chance to, because a moment later Miss Asher bursts back out of her office, flustered. "Did you happen to post any of this on social media?" she asks. "You know, cute cat videos or photographs?"

"About Albert?" I ask, confused.

"Yes. About Albert and the storm, linking one to the other?"

"No."

"Good." She brightens as if relieved. "Excellent. Maybe don't do that, okay?" With no further explanation she dashes back to her office. Joe and I stand there, silent, wondering, at a loss.

"Was she excited or mad?" Joe asks after a minute.

"Excited," I say. "Did you see how her eyes were twitching in her head and she was kind of glowing? It's the same thing that happens when a new book by Margaret Atwood shows up."

"Really?" Joe asks, clearly dazzled by my astute observational skills.

"Totally."

Joe thinks about this. "Good to know," he says.

We stand around being useless and out of sorts, waiting but not knowing what for, wondering if we should knock, realizing all our questions have gone unanswered and now we just have *more* questions, until Joe finally suggests we go to the ice cream shop down the street for chocolate milkshakes. I agree this is a very good idea. Sometimes when things are strange and upside down, a big hit of sugar is the best solution.

Chapter 14

FACT: IF THINGS CAN GET WEIRDER, THEY WILL

WE SIT ON A BENCH at the edge of Community Park, a big green space with soccer fields and baseball diamonds and playgrounds, slurping our frosty milkshakes and throwing out theories about what turned Miss Asher up to a Margaret Atwood level of excitement.

"We didn't even get to ask her our cat questions," Joe says.

"Something about Albert set her off," I reply. "She took that old notebook and basically ran away."

"It's all very bizarre."

In silence we consider just how very bizarre, until Joe says, "I bet Albert is really CIA."

"He's a *cat*," I say pointedly, taking a long pull on my straw. The icy drink temporarily numbs my sinuses, and my eye winks shut against the chill.

"Brain freeze," I whisper.

"Oh, I hate those."

"Any other ideas?" I ask.

"Nope."

"Come on, let's walk. I think better when I'm moving."

We wind through the neighborhoods between the library and my house, streets lined with small ranch houses, some three-story apartment buildings filled with college students, and a long commercial strip with a gas station and a supermarket. The pavement is shiny with the most recent rain, and the air carries a hint of salty ocean.

At the next intersection, Joe slows down. "What is the grief over?" he asks. His question stops me fast. "Miss Asher said Albert might help you with your grief."

Normally when people ask me about Dad, my whole body shuts down. But instead, the words exit hot and sharp from my mouth before I even know they are coming. "My dad died. He got hit by a car."

Joe's gaze jerks up, searching my face. "I'm sorry," he whispers.

The giant lump in my throat that usually only comes

around when I am dealing with Mom makes an unexpected appearance. My eyes bulge with the pressure of tears wanting to burst out. In all these months, not a single kid has said they are sorry about my dad. None of the students at Washington Middle School. Not even Mia. It hits me like a punch to the gut, and for a moment I'm glued to the sidewalk. Joe steps off the curb.

"Let's go see Albert," he says, gesturing at me to come on. I follow him, the lump growing bigger. Joe *must* be my friend, because he knows not to look too closely at me right now. At this moment, with my lumpy throat and the pressure behind my eyes, I do not want to be seen.

We are two blocks away when the sky suddenly darkens. The gray clouds thicken. Rain begins to fall in sheets. Oh no. Here we go again.

"This keeps happening," Joe groans. We break into a run, sprinting the rest of the way to my house while the wind whips into a frenzy around us. The milkshake sloshes around in my stomach. When I throw open the door to the house, we are hit by the unmistakable stink of burned plastic.

I take the lead, darting toward my bedroom. For a split second, before I go in, I'm afraid of what I will find. But this is *Albert*. My kitten. My friend. I shove the door open, and the smell grows stronger.

"*Cassie*," Joe whispers. Yes. I totally get it. Albert is fine, frolicking in his water bowl like some sort of fuzzy duck, stomping down on the water to make a splash and swatting at it as it arcs through the air. He is joyful, happy, and undeniably pleased with himself.

But none of this explains the *steam*. Great, billowing clouds of it are coming off the bowl as if the water inside is at a slow boil.

Joe grips the doorjamb. "There is no way that he can be agitating the water fast enough to create steam," he hisses. "It's just physically . . . *impossible*."

Yet all these things that can't happen *keep* happening. The storms, the scorching dumpster, the spontaneous combustion, the red eyes, a bowl of boiling water. Outside, the wind builds.

"Do you think he's causing the storms?" I ask, understanding my question is completely out of left field. He's a tiny kitten! Not some dark lord of the weather!

I take a step closer, and Albert finally notices us. Leaping up, he springs in our direction, clearly delighted we are here. I scoop him up, half expecting his body to burn my hands, but all I feel is damp fur. Joe rushes to the bowl to inspect it, forehead creased in concentration. Albert nuzzles my neck with wet whiskers and purrs while my heart races double time. I glance around the room, looking for more burn marks or other oddities, and my eyes fall on the half-open closet door.

It's not a pristine-white door. There are scuff marks along the bottom and dings in the paint. There is also the faded outline of a hand turkey I drew in purple marker back when I was in second grade. But now there is something else there too. It's a symbol, scratched into the door about six inches off the floor. In front of the door on the carpet are what look to be a few tiny iridescent seashells, like mini versions of the abalone shells Dad and Mom and me used to collect on the beach. And I am *sure* neither of these things was here this morning.

"Joe," I say, gesturing. "Look at that."

"I'm already looking," he says. "Tell me you carved that with a fork when you were five and got in trouble."

I shake my head. "It's new."

"As in you are seeing it with fresh eyes?" Joe asks hopefully.

"As in it was not here this morning," I hiss. "Neither were those shells or whatever."

Joe nudges them with his toe. "Scales," he mutters. "They look like *scales*."

"What?"

"Never mind. This is just great. The glowing, steaming, weather-manipulating kitten is also an artist? A feline cave painter?"

In my arms, Albert wiggles as if thrilled his skill is appreciated. I giggle. I can't help it. It just rises out of me like soda from a shaken can.

"Why are you *laughing*?" Joe asks. "Don't laugh. This is *not* funny. I mean, what is next? Unicorns falling from the sky?" Oh, he had to go and say "unicorns," which right now is the funniest word I have ever heard in my whole life.

Joe narrows his gaze, a second away from scolding me. "This is a serious situation, Cassie. Get a grip."

I hold up a hand, tears sliding down my cheeks. "Okay. I know. I'm sorry. I'm good. What do you think it is?"

We get up right close to the scratching. Albert looks from me to Joe and back to me again, like he is waiting for feedback on his work. The image, about eight inches in diameter, is a double circle. The inner circle has detail that makes it look like a flat planet Earth. In the space between the inner and outer circles is a series of stars. I run my fingers over it, feeling the grooves and bumps.

"I don't know what it is," Joe responds. Pulling out his phone, he snaps a bunch of pictures, close up and at different angles. "Do you suppose someone broke in here and did it while we were at school? But wait, wouldn't your mom have heard them?"

I shrug. "Probably not." Definitely not. When Mom downs a couple of those pills, our house could be swept up in a tornado and she would not wake up. It's another thing that used to scare me but I am now used to.

"Symbols are pretty universal," Joe says, scratching his head. "Like, you see the same ones across cultures and things. It's hardwired into our brains or something. Let me do some research and see if I can find out anything about this one. I'm starting to lose track of all the mysteries we are supposed to be solving."

"The weather. The kitten. The symbol," I say.

He glares at me. "I didn't *really* mean I forgot. I'm going to go home and get to work."

Patting Albert on the head, Joe coos at him in a way that is embarrassing enough that I close my eyes and wait for it to be over. When he's gone, I put one of the small scales or whatever it is on the tip of my finger and study it. It changes color as I move it around in the light, from black to swirly purple and blue to multiple shades of gray to dark green. It's beautiful, almost like a jewel. Still holding the scale, I spend another five minutes staring at the symbol on the closet door. It doesn't mean anything to me. It's just a bunch of lines. But it was done with intent, so it is meant to be *something*.

I'm lost in it when Albert grows impatient and tugs my shoelaces. He's hungry and bored, and I'm not paying enough attention to him.

"Hey," I say, bringing him to eye level. "What's the thing on the door? Did you do that? Are you making the storms?" He cocks his head this way and that, as if following my words. I half expect him to open his little mouth and answer, recognizing that would be amazing but also terrifying. It's okay for animals to talk in Disney movies and all, but this is real life!

Jumping down, Albert saunters out of my room, headed for the kitchen. In just a few days, he is completely at ease and has the routine down. It's dinnertime, which is almost as marvelous as breakfast time. When I don't immediately follow, he returns to my door and meows in complaint.

"Coming!" I say, scurrying after him.

While I heat up some leftover pasta and sauce, I spoon a little bit of kibble and canned cat food in his bowl and mix it together. Impatient, Albert tries to push aside my hand and jam his head into the bowl.

"Just wait," I instruct. He grumbles at me. When the microwave pings, I take my bowl and his bowl and a glass of water to the table. We sit across from each other. Albert scarfs down his food in about thirty seconds and looks at me with relief and desire. He's no longer starving, but he would like some more, please.

"You eat too fast," I say. "Do you even taste your food? No, I don't think you do." Albert sticks his nose into my bowl but decides red sauce is not for him. "Sorry. But that's what's on the menu for tonight. I'll give you a little more food if you promise to eat it slowly."

Does he nod? I think he nods. I add another tablespoon of kibble to his bowl, and, obviously delighted, he plows right in. This time he's done in twenty seconds and, again, eyes me expectantly. Gone is the lost look I thought I kept catching glimpses of.

"Forget it," I say. "No more." Instead of arguing, he crams his entire head into the water glass, his speck of a pink tongue darting into the water and lapping it up. "Don't get stuck."

But I could watch him drink water from my glass all day. In truth, I can barely remember my life before he was in it.

Chapter 15

THE SLEEPOVER

FOR ABOUT TWENTY-FOUR HOURS, nothing weird happens, as in Albert doesn't glow or steam or spontaneously catch on fire. There are no more storms. He's just a regular kitten obsessed with knocking pencils off my desk and leaping onto my head when I'm lying in bed reading. He complains bitterly when I carry him around in the pocket of my hoodie and complains bitterly when I don't. Cats, it seems, are never satisfied. Joe told me that cats share 95.6 percent of their DNA with lions, and the only thing keeping Albert from eating me is his size. But I don't think so. We're friends, and eating your friends is not polite.

At school on Friday, I volunteer to help Mrs. Holmes

clean lab equipment during lunch. It means I get extra credit, but more importantly, it means I don't have to go to the cafeteria and get stuck between blowing off Joe and hurting his feelings and making Mia so mad, she uninvites me to the sleepover. Honestly, pet friends are much easier to manage.

After the last bell, I leave school through a side entrance so as to avoid any conversations with anyone. Joe is nowhere to be seen. I wonder if he's still deep in his research. I could see him going down a rabbit hole and forgetting to eat and drink and stuff. I bolt directly home to prepare for Mia's.

Albert follows me around my room as I fill a duffel bag with sleepover things—my rolled-up sleeping bag, toothbrush and toothpaste, a hairbrush I won't use. I jam a pillow in there too. When I used to sleep over at Mia's all the time, I kept a pillow in her closet, but I'm not counting on it still being there.

After burrowing into the duffel and sniffing the sleeping bag, Albert gives a plaintive wail, as if he has figured out I'm leaving him. When I accepted Mia's invitation, I was just thinking about myself and how happy I was to be let back in. I did not consider Albert's feelings at all, and he is not pleased. He positions himself on top of the duffel and gives me a challenging glare, daring me to move him.

"Come on, smoochie face," I say soothingly. "It's just a night. I'll be back early in the morning, and then I can spend all day with you. I'll leave you some extra treats. You can sleep in the pile of smelly socks if you want."

He turns his back, indicating he does not accept my bribes. I'm supposed to be at Mia's by five o'clock. She lives on the presidential streets, which are as fancy as the national park streets but a little bit older and in the opposite direction. It will take me thirty minutes to walk to Kennedy Drive, lugging my bag and holding an umbrella to keep everything from getting soaked. And asking Mom for a ride is out of the question. She has not been behind the wheel since Dad died.

I really have to get going. Albert watches closely, ears tilted forward, inviting me to offer something better, something worthy of his letting me go for an entire night. He's being annoying, but it is nice to be wanted, anyway. I sit down on the floor next to him and stroke his head.

"I promise I will never leave you again," I say finally. "It will be me and you forever. Is that enough? When I get home tomorrow, we will play with your feather toy and you can have extra food. Okay? Are we good? Can I go now? If you come downstairs with me, I'll give you an early dinner. What do you say?"

I know on some level it is bananas to talk to him, but I can't shake the sense he understands me. With a swish of his tail, he hops off the duffel bag and saunters out the door, ready for me to make good on that early-dinner promise.

I arrive at Mia's last. Despite my best efforts to shelter under the umbrella, I'm still a little bit soggy and my toes are cold. Mrs. Wilson greets me with a hug and the same sad face all adults who knew my dad throw my way. Well, not all. Miss Asher has never once given me the adult sad face.

"We haven't seen you in so long," Mrs. Wilson coos. "Come on in. The girls are in the family room." The presidential street houses have big kitchens and big family rooms, as if the families who live in them want to spend a lot of time together. There is a house over on Eisenhower Street that has a garden my dad envied, with a fountain, carefully placed boulders, and a butterfly bush that seems to burst to life whenever a ray of sunshine manages to find it.

Stop it, Cassie! You're at Mia's! Get it together! Don't think about butterfly bushes!

I leave my bag in the hallway and make my way to the

family room. Tucked into the deep, velvet sectional sofa are Mia, Sadie, Lila, and Ruth, heads together over Lila's phone, giggling. When Mia finally looks up, she registers surprise, and for a hot, horrible moment, I think that maybe I wasn't really invited and showing up here was a huge, humiliating mistake.

But the surprise passes, replaced by something chillier. Disgust? I glance down at my hoodie, stained with water but otherwise clean. Sure, my hair is a mess, but I walked here and it was windy like it is all the time now. Still, my stomach begins to clench, and I acutely miss Albert. I wish he were here. Or I were there with him.

I can't stand here like a dork all day staring at them, so I take a few tentative steps and sit on the edge of the sofa, not too close, on the periphery, but not looming, either. I remember the first time Mia and I watched *Mamma Mia!* right in this very spot, belting out the ABBA songs and twirling around the room, dancing along with the movie stars. I never worried about my hair or hoodies then.

"What are you guys doing?" I ask, appalled at how squeaky my voice is.

Lila, with her back to me, says, "Watching this video Marcus posted on social media. Oh my god, it's so funny. I'm just dying." Sadie giggles, and Ruth asks Lila to play it again. Mia is quiet but smiling. She leans back, making space for me to come closer. I have to maneuver around Sadie's outstretched green cowboy boots to see the small screen.

"Turn up the volume," Ruth demands. I expect to see a kid doing stupid tricks on a skateboard and landing on his head. Or a dog eating peanut butter. Or a cat riding a Roomba. Or even a parrot who learned all the curse words.

But no.

It's *Joe*.

The realization hits me like a bucket of cold water over the head. He's in school, pacing an empty hallway in front of the lockers, muttering to himself and gesturing with his hands as if he is part of a full-on conversation, except he is alone. Adrenaline floods my system. My hands squeeze into fists and my vision narrows. Lila turns up the volume.

It's hard to hear what Joe is saying. I can tell he is working out a problem, something complicated, probably having to do with the symbol or the weather or Albert. And I know this because this is how he does it. But no one else knows that. The kids filming giggle and snort.

"Talking to his invisible friend?" one asks.

"Only kind he's got," the other adds.

"Except that girl in the cafeteria. The loser one."

Me. He means me. *I'm* the loser girl. My cheeks flame hot. Mia looks down at her empty lap. Sadie eyes me. I don't know what to do. The noise in my head is so loud, a roar, and the only word I can hang on to is "Albert." I say it over and over like a mantra.

Albert. Albert. Albert. Albert.

And I swear I hear a voice respond.

Coming, Cassie.

Chapter 16

SLEEPOVER, INTERRUPTED

FROZEN ON THE SOFA, I can feel my heart thrashing against my ribs, and I can barely inhale. Ruth watches me, eyes narrowed, waiting for a reaction. This isn't fun if they don't get something out of it. Lila hits play again. The video starts all over. If only I could figure out a way to leave, short of running out the door and making everything worse. The realization that Mia invited me to this sleepover so they could make fun of me dawns like a red-hot sun.

In the kitchen, adjacent to the family room, Mrs. Wilson hums as she puts frozen pizzas in the oven. She says, "Now, I hope everyone over there is being kind. Kindness matters. Pizza in about a half hour."

"Let's go upstairs," Ruth suggests. Mia nudges me to get up. Somehow my legs move, and I follow the girls up the stairs to Mia's room, with its acres of pink carpet and lace curtains and a queen-sized bed like she's a grown-up already. She has two closets full of clothes, tags still dangling from many of them, and a mirrored white vanity table with a padded chair. The table is scattered with tubes and pencils and bottles of makeup.

There was a time when Mia was not interested in clothes and makeup, when we'd stay up most of the night learning card tricks from a book I had and giggling at how bad we were at them. Or we'd climb the trees in Community Park and hope no one caught us. But that is not now.

The four girls throw themselves on the expansive bed like it's a habit, as if they have done this a million times. I linger in the doorway. Shame squeezes into a tight little ball in the pit of my stomach, growing dense and heavy. What do I do? What would Joe do? I didn't see how many views the video had gotten, but I'm sure Lila has played it a dozen times just by herself. Are there videos of me somewhere on there, too, taken when I wasn't paying attention, picking my nose or pulling my underwear out of my butt or whatever?

I wish I didn't exist. Because if I didn't, I would not be here. Simple.

The girls roll around on the bed, giggling and watching videos, and maybe I *don't* exist, because they are acting as if I am not in the room. A flare of anger erupts in my chest, not at them, but at me. How could I be so *stupid*? Did I really think Mia was coming back to me? For the first time since I walked in the door, my eyes well up.

Oh, I can't cry, not here. They will film it and broadcast it to the world, and my humiliation will bloom, leaving me forever in its shadow.

A sudden clap of thunder shakes the house. For the first time, Lila looks up from her phone. "Is this another one of those stupid storms?" she asks. "They are totally annoying."

"Ugh. Agree," replies Ruth. "They make my hair frizzy."

Beyond the bedroom window, rain comes down hard. The trees whip. The house trembles under the assault of heavy hail. As a bolt of lightning flashes, I catch the outline of something outside the window, balanced on the sill.

It can't be. *Impossible.*

I cover the distance to the window in three giant steps and heave it open with my shoulder. "Albert!"

Balanced outside the window, drenched and trembling,

is my kitten, his eyes glowing red and fierce. I swipe him up and hold him tightly to my chest. What is he doing here? How did he get here? *What* is going on?

This, of course, finally pulls the attention of Mia, Sadie, Ruth, and Lila away from the phone. They stare at me as if I have sprouted another head.

"What is *that*?" Mia points a polished fingernail at me.

"My kitten," I stammer.

"You don't have a kitten," she says, lips pursed. They seem unimpressed that he materialized on the second-story windowsill, out of *nowhere*, during a weather *anomaly*. They are asking the wrong questions!

"I do," I respond. "I just got him. His name is Albert." This cannot be happening. Can. Not.

"Told you she's weird," Sadie says with a smirk. "She packed her kitten in her bag. Sad. S. A. D."

"I didn't," I protest. "He got here somehow on his own. He was *outside*." The words sound absurd even to me, but that does not mean they are not true. A giant wet spot blooms on my hoodie where Albert is pressed to my chest.

"Why did you invite her again?" Ruth asks. She gives Mia a nudge.

"My mom," Mia says with a shrug. "She said I had to."

"You should have lied and said she couldn't come," Lila offers helpfully.

"Well, let's learn from our mistakes for next time," Sadie says with a sly smile. I squeeze Albert, but he wiggles free and leaps down to the carpet. "He's not even cute. He's, like, scrawny and mangy." She regards Albert with distaste. "And what is that smell? Like he's burned or something. Yuck."

She jumps from the bed, and I can see what she is going to do before it happens. It unfolds in my mind in slow motion. Albert is sitting near a pink overnight bag with the name *Sadie* embroidered in golden thread. He's dripping on her stuff, and maybe she's just going to kick the bag out of the way. Or maybe she's going to kick Albert. Without thinking, I throw myself forward, in between her boot and the bag.

The boot connects with the bridge of my nose. There's a crack and a blinding spark of pain. Mia screams. "Her nose!" The world buckles as my vision goes wavy. My hands come away from my face with traces of blood. Mia squats beside me. "You broke her nose!"

A tiny part of me registers satisfaction that Mia is shocked, that she is not just blowing off that Sadie kicked me in the face with her boot and smashed my nose and now blood is dripping on the pretty pink carpet, not to mention ruining my perfectly good hoodie.

But where is Albert? Did he get hurt? I wipe my eyes on my sleeve, trying to see as Mia cries next to me and the girls scream and whine. I must look bad. They are really freaking out.

A sudden sharp clap of thunder rings out. It feels like it is coming from *inside* the house. The air fills with smoke. "What the . . ." Sadie coughs and gags and steps back. I scramble to my knees, scanning the room for my kitten.

"Albert!" The haze burns my eyes, but I can see Mia beside me well enough. Her face is frozen, as if she has seen something terrible—or wonderful. I grab her by the shirt. "Where's my *cat*?" I demand.

Mia raises a trembling finger and points into the smoke. And from the cloud emerges a leathery snout filled with razor-sharp teeth, eyes blazing red and furious, wings sleek and black, long tail thrashing the floor in fury.

There is a *dragon* in Mia's room, and I *think* the dragon is Albert.

Chapter 17

DRAGON

MY KITTEN IS A DRAGON. That dragon is my kitten. Maybe, but my brain refuses to accept either possibility and is instead filled with the noise of my heart smashing into my ribs, racing so fast, I think it might burst out of my chest. This isn't real. That boot must have gotten me in the head. But it feels real. Either way, I can't move.

Sadie doesn't move either, her eyes wide as saucers. Lila quivers and shakes, the phone clutched in her hand ready to fly from her grip. Ruth clings to Lila. Mia wraps her arms around her knees as if trying to disappear. I get it. I really do. We are all completely still.

The dragon isn't enormous like the ones that span the sky in books or movies. He's the size of a Great Dane, if you don't include a long, snapping tail ending in a sharp, triangular point. Flames leap from his mouth as he takes one stride toward Ruth, Sadie, and Lila, huddled together, blinking rapidly as if to clear this fantastical, impossible vision. The dragon stretches out his neck so his face is inches from Sadie, who, I think, has actually stopped breathing. She squeezes her eyes shut and recoils.

"Please don't hurt me," she whimpers. I'm impressed her voice works. I'm not sure I could squeak out a single syllable right now. My tongue feels swollen and useless in my mouth. The noise of my heart in my head is almost unbearable.

The dragon inches closer to Sadie. Their noses practically touch. Sadie sweats, the beads rolling down from her temples like raindrops. The dragon's skin is black and shiny, overlaid with scales infused with a pearly iridescence, the bedroom light illuminating different shades and depths of color. His wings, tucked tightly against his body, ripple and flex. Hot waves wash onto us as he breathes in and out. I have never seen anything so beautiful.

"I . . . I didn't mean it," Sadie whispers, her voice quavering. "I was just moving my bag."

In response the dragon snarls. The scent of singed hair

fills the air. His lips curl back, and flames leak out between his razor-sharp teeth. He smacks his tail on the floor twice. The message is clear.

Enough is enough.

"What is happening up here?" It's Mrs. Wilson, hysterical, running up the stairs.

"Is something on fire?" Mr. Wilson bellows. He's hot on her heels. "Are you girls all right?"

I survey the scene. A dragon, blood all over the carpet, my smashed face, Sadie's burned hair. I'd say the answer to Mr. Wilson's question is no, we are not all right. None of this is going to be easy to explain. Part of me wants to giggle. I recognize that part as shock. I'm unraveling.

And somehow, during the time it takes to glance from the bedroom door back to Albert, he's returned to kitten form, curled in a ball and dead asleep. The dragon is gone. The girls, all four of them, start crying. But the urge to giggle is gone. My head is clear.

I need to get out of here.

I grab Albert and stuff him in my pocket. Mr. and Mrs. Wilson tumble into the room. The wailing girls throw themselves forward, screaming. Mr. Wilson aims a fire extinguisher hose at the room and just starts spraying. Mrs. Wilson pulls the girls into her arms. It's chaos. This is my chance. I dodge around Mrs. Wilson and the girls, down the stairs, and out of the house. I don't even bother to grab my stuff, which sits where I dumped it, as if it knew I would not be staying.

With one hand on Albert to keep him secure, I run. I run until my lungs burn from the effort and my cheeks sting from the rain and my head aches from my bruised nose. I run through Community Park, avoiding the pools of brightness thrown off by the streetlamps, across the deserted soccer fields, and by the scorched live oak. It doesn't make sense, but the harder I run, the calmer my insides feel.

I finally stop when I reach Rainbow City, an expansive playground with climbing towers and giant slides, zip lines, and wobbly bridges. Hunkering down on one of the covered benches, I try to stop my shaking hands.

I want to talk to Joe. I wish he were here.

Slowly, a little afraid, I pull Albert from my pocket and bring him right up to my face. He snoozes, tail wrapped over his little nose to keep it warm. "What happened back there?" I whisper. "Was that *you*? It *was* you, wasn't it? What are you? *Who* are you?"

He opens one eye, scans the scene as if looking for food,

and seeing none forthcoming, closes his eye and goes back to snoozing.

I don't understand. I don't understand anything. I am missing major pieces of important information.

My kitten turned into a dragon, right in Mia's bedroom. I can't help but laugh, but that really hurts my nose. "Ouch." I touch the puffy skin with a finger and wince. This night has not gone the way I thought it would. "I'm glad it was me and not you," I say, stroking Albert's damp fur. "Those boots sure do hurt."

I wonder what is happening at the Wilsons' house right now. Are they trying to talk the girls out of the idea that they saw a dragon because the idea that they *did* see a dragon is just plain crazy? Will the girls start to doubt that they did actually see a dragon? Will they blame me for the smoke and singed hair and for harboring a fantastic beast? What if they come after me and I get in trouble? What if they take Albert *away*?

The questions swirl, like their own tornado. My heart, which had finally settled down, begins to race. Heat floods my body. I might lose Albert. Not good. Really not good.

I need to see Joe. Joe will have answers.

I tuck Albert back into my pocket and head for the

national park streets. One seventy-five Acadia, he said. At Joe's house, outside lights brighten the whole yard as if welcoming any passing stranger to stop by and say hello. But I can't just knock. My face is a mess, and I'm carrying a dragon in my pocket.

A giggle swells in my chest. *Not now, Cassie! Keep it together!*

Right. Okay. I search around until I find a few small rocks. If Joe is in his room, this might work. But how do I know which room is his? I've never been in his house, as we haven't been friends for very long. Joe did mention he shares a bedroom with his brother Andrew, who just happens to be captain of the Washington Middle School soccer team and unaware that I exist, and I also know that the bedroom faces the street.

Picking up a small chip of broken sidewalk, I figure I have a fifty-fifty chance of getting the right window. There are additional variables as well, like: Is Joe even in his room? What if Andrew hears the noise? The right window has a neatly drawn purple curtain. No way Joe and Andrew share a room with a neatly drawn curtain. Winding up, I hurl the tiny piece of sidewalk at the left window. It connects perfectly, like I might be a Major League Baseball secret weapon or something. Possibly too perfectly. *Clink!*

A spider's web of tiny cracks spreads from where the concrete chip made contact. Oops. Pulling my hood up, I slink down the sidewalk. What was I thinking, throwing rocks at windows?

"Cassie!" Joe stands in his front door, too-big track pants drooping from his narrow hips. "What the heck? Oh man, what *happened* to you?"

My fingers float to my nose, tender and swollen. "Sadie kicked me with a green cowboy boot," I say flatly. Now that I am here, I don't know where to begin.

"She what?"

"Kicked me," I repeat.

Joe glances up and down the empty street, as if he half expects to see Sadie and her green boots headed our way. "You better come inside," he says. "I think you need an ice pack."

The door swings open, releasing a blast of warm scented air. Piles of tennis shoes and backpacks and random socks and shin guards and empty shipping boxes headed for the recycle bin spread out like water on the floor. Jackets and hoodies bulge from hooks lining the walls.

As I pick my way through the minefield of stuff, Joe says, "Mom and Dad and Bryant and Lane and Aidan and Andrew went to the basketball game." It's funny he lists them all, like an inventory or a memory game. "I'm not a fan."

The house smells of an intoxicating mix of cotton-candy sweetness, ginger, nutmeg, and butter. I follow Joe to an expansive kitchen flowing into a family room, complete with a scattering of chairs and a giant television. The acres of kitchen island are laden with two pies, a frosted coconut layer cake that looks like a dream, a tray of blueberry muffins, and several piles of cookies, teetering like cartoon towers.

"My mom is an architect," Joe explains, gesturing to the spread of baked goods. "When she's trying to work a problem, like puzzle it out, she bakes. She's working on a bridge right now. It's complicated. Which means soon she will be baking bread. Complicated problems always end up with bread." He shrugs. "Help yourself. We have two freezers full in the garage already."

Joe fills a ziplock bag with ice and hands it to me. I have not yet mentioned the dragon, that Albert *is* a dragon, that Sheldon Slack might just be right. This seems like what I should have led with. I slap the ice pack to my face. First contact hurts so much, I yelp.

"You better start at the beginning," Joe says, pulling two pies close and studying them. "It seems like the kind of story that might require pie. Do you like apple or peach?"

Peach. And he doesn't know the half of it.

Chapter 18

YOU WILL NOT BELIEVE THIS. I BARELY BELIEVE THIS.

I SHIFT THE ICE PACK AROUND on my face, trying to find a comfortable position. It turns out there isn't one. Joe waits, tapping his foot impatiently, while shoveling warm peach pie into his mouth. "So?" he prompts.

"Promise me you won't say anything until I'm done?" I ask. My voice is all nasally from my injured nose.

Joe puts his fork down slowly. "Okay," he says. "I promise. Go ahead."

I begin with the invite to the sleepover, how I had just seen Sheldon Slack across from City Hall when Mia and her friends showed up.

"Why did you say yes?" Joe asks.

"You said you wouldn't interrupt," I reply.

"But she's mean to you." When he says it, it seems so simple, not representative of the complicated feelings that churn around in my gut when it comes to Mia. And I haven't even gotten to the bad part yet.

"It's actually worse than me just going to her house," I say. "Now be quiet."

Joe grumbles but stuffs his mouth with pie. When I get to the part about the video on Lila's phone, the video of *him*, I pause, unsure how to explain that I didn't defend him. I didn't stand up and demand they cease and desist, and I didn't leave the party on principle. But the weight of it is too much, so I just tell the truth. "There was a video of you," I say quietly. "On social media. You were talking to yourself in the hallway, and the kids who filmed it, well, they were saying things. Mia and those guys were playing it over and over."

Joe casts his eyes down at his feet. "Did you get kicked because you tried to defend me?"

This question cuts deep. No. I didn't say *anything*. But next time, if there *is* a next time, I swear I will. Instead of telling him that, I sidestep. "We ended up in Mia's bedroom," I continue. "And then one of those storms happened."

"Oh yeah," Joe says, spraying pie crumbs all over the place. "That was right when everyone was leaving for the game! Mom said that we might have to move if this keeps up. She finds little tornadoes popping up all over the place unsettling."

"Yeah. But this is the part where it gets kind of . . . strange." Understatement of the year! I explain how Albert appeared at Mia's bedroom window, two stories up, out of nowhere.

Joe can no longer contain himself. "How did he get there? How did he know how to find Mia's house? That is one hundred percent impossible!"

Wait until he hears the rest. He won't have a percentage for how impossible it is. "You said you wouldn't ask questions until I was done," I say. "But you keep doing it."

"I did. Sorry. Go on."

"Where was I? Albert appeared. Somehow he was there, and the girls started to give me a hard time about him. They thought I brought him with me or something. And then he got too close to Sadie's bag, and there was Sadie in her green boots, and I thought she was going to kick him. So I jumped between them."

"And got a boot to the nose," Joe interrupts.

"Clearly. But that's not the point. Something else

happened. Something . . . unimaginable." I pull Albert out of my pocket and hold him to my chest. He sleeps soundly, content as can be, tiny and soft and perfect.

"What?" Joe asks.

"Albert," I say slowly. "He's a *dragon*. He *turned* into a dragon. Right there in front of me. There was thunder and smoke, and then there was a *dragon*."

Joe's fork clatters to the counter. His mouth gapes. Albert's eyes shoot open, and his body tenses. "He *what*?"

"He turned into a dragon."

"He did not."

"He did."

"I don't believe it."

"I don't really believe it either, but I saw it happen."

"Can you make him do it again?"

"I don't know how it works."

"Okay. Sorry. I had to ask!" Joe begins pacing the length of the kitchen, muttering to himself, like in the video. "For the record, I believe you."

"You do?"

He eyes me. "Of course I do. We're friends. You have no reason to lie to me."

I'm flooded with relief. I like Joe's version of friendship.

It makes sense, and it doesn't tie my stomach up in knots.

"Thank you for believing me," I say quietly. We eat some more pie. I'm not sure what sort of conversation people are supposed to have after the world has turned upside down.

"So we have to consider the possibility," Joe says finally, "that Slack was telling the truth. The storms are linked to . . . um . . . dragons. I honestly can't believe I just said that out loud with a straight face."

I don't argue. Now that I've seen a dragon, I'm in no position to say something is impossible. Suddenly *everything* seems possible. I would not be surprised to stick my head out the front door and see a bunch of unicorns prancing down the street. Or the Loch Ness Monster swimming by. Or Bigfoot out for a stroll. A trickle of freezing water from the ice bag runs down my chin.

"What do we do?" I ask. "What if the Wilsons tell the police and they come after me and want to take Albert? I think he burned Sadie's hair." I remember that scene in *The Wizard of Oz* where Miss Gulch takes Toto away. But the little dog escapes and returns to Dorothy straightaway. Dorothy is no dummy. She knows Miss Gulch will be back, and the next time Toto might not be so lucky. She runs away to save her dog.

But I'm thinking, if they come for my dragon, there might not be a second chance. I might have to get away from Lewiston right *now*.

Joe stops pacing. "Okay. Let's say the storms and Albert are connected. And Albert is a dragon."

"Okay. We can say that."

"And Albert carved that symbol in the closet door." I'd forgotten all about the symbol. It seems like such a long time ago that we found it.

"Right," I respond. "The symbol."

"Well, I've gone deep on it," Joe says. "There is this group of, like, extra-nerdy nerds that I belong to. I know you might find that weird." No. Not at all. Not one bit. "Anyway, we help each other understand things that aren't understandable, you know, like the symbol. We're kind of like detectives."

He pauses to pull open the refrigerator, grabs a container of orange juice, and chugs right from it. I pull what remains of the pie closer to me. I missed dinner, and despite all the excitement, my stomach is still on a schedule. Putting Albert gently on the counter, I ask, "And?"

Joe grins. "I told them how you and I had lived through the first freak storm together and we're now, like, best friends, and that we found the symbol at your house because we hang out all the time together. They all thought that was pretty excellent."

"But did they know what the symbol was?" I ask.

"Well, my nerdy nerd peeps had a lot of ideas. One girl said the symbol might be plans for an alien spaceship, which I considered for a few minutes." Wait, alien *spaceships*? "There were theories about an ancient Maya civilization communicating with the present. Also, that the paint on the door was somehow defective. We covered a lot of ground. But none of it was helpful, to be honest."

"So why are you telling me?"

"Hang on, I'm getting to it. One of my friends on there, Emily, likes to say that the best way to figure out a problem is to change your point of view, you know, to look at the situation *differently*. Like, if you look at a redwood tree from the ground, it looks way different than if you look at it from the sky. The tree is exactly the same, it's just the point of view is different."

He takes another pull on the orange juice, wiping his mouth on his sleeve. "So I *stretched* it."

"You what?"

"I stretched the symbol!" he shouts. "I took the image and rendered it in three dimensions. You know what that is, right?"

"Yes," I snap. "No need to be insulting."

"Just checking. Never know."

"Go on."

"Right. Anyway. 3D." His eyes twinkle. "It was like a flat balloon suddenly filled with air. And, wow, it turns into this sphere with all sorts of details. And you know what?"

I'll admit I'm holding my breath. "No. What?"

"The stars are the constellations, and they point to various places on Planet Earth!" Joe throws up his arms, apparently forgetting he's still holding the container. Sticky orange juice sprays in all directions. "It's a freaking *map*!"

Chapter 19

THE SYMBOL

ALBERT'S EARS ROTATE like satellites when Joe starts throwing orange juice and yelling. He edges right up to Joe on the counter and stares at him, as if egging him on to do something. Joe stares back. "I feel like he is trying to tell me something," he says. "Or maybe he's going to eat me."

I do not mention how I felt Albert in my head earlier. That detail, small as it may be, feels like too much to share at the moment. "Can I see the map?" I ask.

Joe races off, returning moments later with an iPad. The image on the screen is a three-dimensional Earth as seen from space. Surrounding the blue orb are clusters of yellow stars. Dotted lines lead from the stars to various points around the world. Joe taps the screen and spins the planet.

"The lines go to certain places," Joe explains, zooming in on a line leading from the stars to a spot near Mount Fuji in Japan. He spins the globe again to a line leading to an area outside of London. Still another to a cluster of islands off Greece. There are lines to tropical Australia, Botswana in Africa, and the very tip of Argentina in South America.

And one leading to the Arcata wilderness, hundreds of miles of deep, thick forest, just north of *Lewiston*.

I point. "That's right here."

"I know," Joe says with a nod. "It was impossible to tell from the flat image." He taps the screen, and the original version, the one from the closet door, appears. But it retains the color that Joe added. It looks like a stained glass window.

I gasp. "This is the symbol on the cover of Miss Asher's notebook," I yelp. "The one she keeps in the locked drawer."

"Are you sure?"

"Pretty sure. Yes. Totally sure."

Joe sets his lips in a tight determined line. "That cannot be a coincidence. Maybe what is in that notebook will help us understand what this is a map *to*, exactly. And maybe then everything will make sense." Outside, a car door slams shut. "Oh, shoot. They're home. Okay. Let's meet tomorrow morning when the library opens at nine. We'll get the note-book and start figuring stuff out. And when we know what is going on, we will know what to do. Deal?"

My instinct is to run, but what Joe is saying makes sense. The more we know, the better off we are. I sneak out the back door to avoid explaining to Joe's family why my nose is bruised or the fact that I am in possession of a dragon.

I cover the ground between Joe's house and mine in record time. I half expect a fleet of police cars, lights swirl-ing, sirens blaring, to be parked out front, but all is quiet in the neighborhood. I told my mother I was going to sleep over at Mia's, but did she hear me? I can't be sure. Before I creep into the house, I formulate a story about skateboard-ing, not very well, and hitting my nose on the sidewalk curb. It's not an airtight story, but it will have to do. Taking a deep breath that hurts my face, I slip inside.

It's only eight thirty, but Mom is asleep on the couch with the TV mindlessly droning on. Albert jumps from his kangaroo pouch and immediately charges to his food bowl, throwing me a look of deep displeasure when he finds it empty. Clearly, transforming into a dragon takes a lot of energy and requires a second dinner.

"Hold on. I'm on it." I toss crunchy kibble and some

canned food together and set it before him. He shoves his whole face into the bowl. Is this the right meal for a dragon? Can Albert fly? Are *all* cats dragons? That would be interesting . . . and terrifying. Or is my cat the only dragon? Where did he come from? What is he doing here? Is he lost? Does he not know how to get home? Is that why he sometimes looks so sad? These questions leave me a little dizzy, and I clutch the counter to make sure I don't tumble to the floor. Over the sink, I catch my reflection in the window. Wow. My nose is puffy, and I am sporting a black eye. There is dried blood on my cheek around a small cut. Seeing my injuries somehow makes them hurt worse, so I look away, suddenly weary right down to my bones.

This is when my sleeping mother, now very much awake, appears in the doorway. There is no way to hide my face. I mean, I can't stick it in a pocket like an injured finger or anything. For a flash I think she won't notice. But no such luck. Her face, usually so blank, suddenly animates. "Who did this to you?" she says, her voice gravelly from underuse. Tension creates a tight expression, her lips pressed together, eyes narrowed.

I'll admit, she looks a little scary, but also *awake*. It startles me.

"Skateboard!" I blurt. "Joe was teaching me tricks, and it

turns out I'm not very good. I landed on the curb nose-first."

Her fists unfurl. "You need to be more careful," she says quietly. And then, almost as an afterthought, "It's just you and me now." Another moment passes until she commands I sit down so she can clean up my face. She finds an ancient bag of peas in the freezer, and I press them to my nose. She doesn't ask about Mia's, probably because she forgot I was supposed to be there, but her focus on my face is complete. The startled feeling morphs into hope. Is she coming back to me?

Don't, Cassie! You'll only be disappointed.

This is true. I fix my eyes on Albert, who snoozes on the floor, one paw in his food bowl and his tail draped over his water bowl, as if he were too tired to even move an inch to the side before he fell asleep. I notice a few gray hairs on the soft space of his cheeks that were not there before.

Finally Mom sends me to bed. I scoop up my kitten, and without bothering to brush my teeth or change my clothes, I fall into bed, tucking Albert tightly into my belly. This day was really too much.

Sleep comes fast, like a black tidal wave, and the dream that follows is so vivid, I am sure it is actually happening. I'm in a forest; light streams through the towering trees, catching the lingering mist and casting a magical glittery glow. I can feel the damp breeze on my skin, the pale sun on my shoulders. I smell lilacs and something like melted candle wax. It could be the Arcata wilderness, but something is not right. The purple butterflies are the size of dinner plates and sparkle too brightly. And the trees themselves are iridescent, reflecting like a million tiny mirrors.

Albert is with me but in his dragon form. "Where are we?" I ask.

"Don't know, Cassie," Albert replies. There is nothing unusual about a talking dragon in my dream. Albert scans the trees, searching. Soon, from the forest emerges a brilliant silver dragon. She is so dazzling that I can barely look at her. She gazes at Albert with love and longing, and tears prick the corners of my eyes. Somewhere there is a dragon who is heartbroken at his loss, who fears him missing or dead, who is maybe searching for him right now.

"Is this your mother?" I ask.

"Yes, Cassie," Albert breathes.

The silver dragon flaps her mighty wings a single time and lands right before us, but I'm not scared. She intends me no harm. She wraps Albert in those wings so completely that he disappears. She smells of sunshine and pine trees, a wonderful heady concoction that makes me weak in the knees.

But this is a dream, Cassie!

Is it? It feels so real! Like the images have been delivered directly into my head, not generated by me. I reach out a hand and touch the silver dragon. My fingers come away covered in rainbow iridescence. The silver dragon turns to me, her eyes warm and grateful. Albert peeks his head out. His face glows with happiness. I can feel his contentment deep in my own chest. I recognize this feeling, but only because I don't have it anymore. He's *home*.

"Albert, are you home?" I ask. "Is this home?"

"Home, Cassie," he replies.

"How do we get here, Albert?" I ask urgently. "Where are we and how do we get here?"

But before Albert can answer, I wake with a start, my body soaked with sweat. The clock reads two a.m., and while I'm sure I'm awake, everything still feels hazy, the dream clinging like a sticky cobweb. Albert sits on my chest, eyes wide open, as if staring into my brain.

"Do you want to go home?" I whisper, my fingers plunged deep into his fur. He cocks his head to the left and blinks. Then he leaps off me and scampers to the closet door, plopping down in front of the symbol that we now know is a map and sitting there for a beat before returning to the bed. He locks eyes with me, expectant.

He said he wanted to go home.

My breath catches fast in my throat. But where *is* home? Albert didn't even know in the dream! It was just a pretty forest, not exactly a specific place with specific directions. And how badly can he want to go there if he can't even remember where it is? I mean, maybe he's like a human baby who would not be able to tell you where she lives either, but that is not the point.

What about *me*? If he goes home, I'm left here, and how can I exist without him? Albert watches me closely. I don't understand, and I don't even really want to. I shove the dream and the thought of it aside.

Albert pushes his head into my chin. But as I pull him into my chest, I swear I see a wisp of sparkles trail from my fingers.

Chapter 20

RUNAWAY

THE NEXT DAY, Albert paws me awake as a faint edge of light creeps up on the horizon. He wants his breakfast. He does not care that I slept poorly, plagued by anxiety from what happened at Mia's and wonder at the message of the dream. There is a moment before I'm fully conscious when it's possible to believe that none of it actually happened. But when I roll over and my nose hits the pillow, I know it did. Ow! I gingerly press my fingers into my face. The swelling has gone down, but the tenderness underneath remains. Just in case, I check my fingertips for signs of sparkles, but there are none.

Albert meows pitifully. He's hungry. Grumbling, I heave myself out of my warm bed. Outside the sky is showing signs of being gray and overcast but calm. No lightning and thunder, no hail or rain or wind, no tornadoes. I pad first to the bathroom to check out my face. The black eye is prominent, but my nose is almost back to normal size. The slice on my cheek is a crusty scab that, while kind of gross, doesn't actually hurt that much. I look like I got in a fight and lost. Albert swats at my bare feet, impatient with this side trip.

In the kitchen, I pour a bowl of cereal for myself while Albert wolfs down his food. An image of the silver dragon from the dream intrudes on my breakfast. No. Forget it. I'm not thinking about that. Albert belongs here with me, and that is that. So what that he is a dragon? He's *my* dragon.

But what happened at the Wilsons' will have a fallout. Did they call the police? Will those FBI agents who investigate weird stuff hunt me down? Will they take Albert? I shudder. We have to go to the library, read that notebook, learn everything we possibly can, and then Albert and I need to get out of Lewiston. I have thirty dollars in my sock drawer from doing odd jobs for old Mrs. Cowie across the street. It's not much, but it will buy a bus ticket out of here. I decide not to think about where I will go and what I will do when I get there because I have no idea.

The landline phone, sitting on the counter next to the toaster, rings and jolts me from these thoughts. I lunge for it before it wakes up my mother. "Hello?"

"Hello, this is Detective Rhodes from the Lewiston PD. I'm trying to reach a Mrs. Jones."

Without even thinking, I say, "This is Mrs. Jones."

"Good morning, ma'am. Sorry to bother you on a Saturday morning, but I have a few questions about, ah, your daughter, a one Cassandra Jones."

"What about her?" I interrupt, my pulse leaping.

"This might sound a little . . . odd . . . but we have a report here that she may be in possession of an exotic animal. Exotic animals are not, ah, legal here in California. Do you happen to know anything about this?"

An exotic animal? What? Albert is not an exotic animal. He's a *dragon*. "No, I do not," I say flatly.

"She was apparently at a friend's house last night and there was an . . . incident," the detective says. "I have a statement from Gary Wilson. Fire may have been involved."

"I don't know what you are talking about," I say quickly. "She was here with me last night. We were watching television."

Detective Rhodes pauses. "Perhaps it would be best if you came down here and we could have a chat. Would that be all right?" Yes. That would be great. They will be sitting there waiting for my mother to show up, and by the time they figure out what has happened, I will be long gone.

"How about after lunch?" I suggest.

"Great," replies Detective Rhodes. "Just ask for me when you get here."

I hang up, glancing at the clock. Forty-five minutes until I need to meet Joe. No matter what we find in that notebook, staying in Lewiston is no longer an option. I can only imagine what the Wilsons said in their report, but with the burned hair, it's probably not something the police will forget. Fortunately, forty-five minutes is plenty of time to throw some belongings into a bag and prepare to run away.

Chapter 21

VIRAL VIDEO

I MEET JOE ON THE CORNER of my street. He struggles under an unusually full backpack. It is practically bursting at the seams. "I'm going with you," he says, unprompted.

"Where?" I ask.

"To run away," he replies.

"I never said anything about running away," I say.

"You didn't have to," he responds. "It's what I would do."

I think about his kitchen and the peach pie. Why would he want to run away? For Dorothy in *The Wizard of Oz*, it ended up being pretty fantastic, but also terrifying. "I think . . ."

He holds up a hand. "Don't try to talk me out of it. It won't work."

"Thanks," I say quietly, a warm fuzzy feeling filling the pit in my stomach.

"Yeah. Whatever. We got problems. Big ones." He pulls up an app on his phone and hands it over. "Look what's trending."

Not having a phone, I don't spend time on social media, as in I don't even have an account, which means I stand there like a dork with no idea how to check what is trending. Joe sighs. It seems less out of exasperation and more because he feels sorry for me. "Upper right-hand corner. The menu."

I click the three lines and a menu drops down. I select "trending" and immediately wish that I hadn't.

#dragons

#DragonHunting

#LewistonGroundZero

My hands shake. I look up at Joe. "I don't understand. How do they *know*?"

"Open the other window," Joe says. "The video." The image frozen on the initial shot of the video is familiar. Pink carpet. Lace curtains. White vanity table. Mia's bedroom. My skin goes clammy. I already know what I'm going to see. But I hit play anyway.

Time is obliterated as the video unspools. Each second feels like a hundred. And while I wanted to bend time, to ride it like a wave, this is not what I meant. Lila shot the video on her new phone. She probably thought she could get a video of me embarrassing myself with my stowaway kitten and put it right up there with the one of Joe talking to himself, a gallery of fools to be laughed at.

But it is much worse.

Smoke fills the frame. There is screaming. I hear my voice with a desperate edge, calling Albert's name. And then he emerges from the cloud, the golden blaze on his chest like a circle of fire, a terrifying image, otherworldly, *impossible*.

"How can people believe this is true?" I stammer. "Videos are faked *all* the time."

"People believe a lot of things that aren't true if they show up on social media," Joe replies. "And then other people tell them they are right for believing something that isn't true, and it just snowballs. An echo chamber. This thing went viral in a hurry. I tried to stop it, but it was too far gone."

I want to panic, to cry and yell and have a proper tantrum about how unfair the world is. Why does everything always have to be so *hard*? But I know throwing a fit will not help. It will only make things worse. So I steel myself for what has to be done.

"We go to the library," I say with a grimace. "We see what's in that notebook, and then we get out of here." Knowing as much as we possibly can about Albert is now urgently important. I can't protect him if I don't understand what is happening.

"My thoughts exactly." We hitch up our extra-heavy backpacks, I give Albert a squeeze in my pocket, and we head to the library.

It's a normal volunteer day, so our being there won't be suspicious as long as Miss Asher has not been on social media. I vaguely remember her telling me she thought social media would bring on the eventual apocalypse, which means she probably doesn't hang out on there too much. However, the question of how we are going to get Miss Asher to give us the notebook remains unanswered.

"We could just tell her everything," I suggest. "And ask to see the notebook."

"Remember how she wigged out over just a few details? No way."

Oh. Yeah. Right. "How about I distract her and you break into the drawer? We'll just borrow the book for a minute and then put it back. It's a library. Borrowing is kind of the whole point."

"Great idea." Joe nods. "How about *I* distract her and *you* get the book? I like the chances of that working better."

"Why me?" I demand, stepping off the curb and into the bike lane without looking. Joe yanks me back just before a bicycle plows me under.

"Be careful!" he reprimands. "And it's because you are braver than I am. You crawled in that dumpster." He shivers at the memory. I'm flattered, but also I feel like I've been had, because here I am agreeing to break into the drawer and take the notebook. Trying to be helpful, Joe describes a video he watched once of a girl picking a lock with a paper clip.

"Or maybe it was a bobby pin? You know, for hair? I can't remember."

Great. This is off to a fantastic start. "Maybe I'll just yank it really hard," I suggest.

"You *are* pretty strong," Joe says in all seriousness. "Will that work?"

"Well, it is probably just as good an idea as a bobby pin," I snap. "I mean, do you *see* any bobby pins lying around?"

He peers at my hair. "Nope. But I bet there are paper clips on Miss Asher's desk."

"What are the odds this works?" I ask him.

He shrugs. "Oh, I'd give us a thirty percent chance of success, give or take."

What? I don't like those odds. Joe grins. I will say one thing about him: he does not give up, even when the outlook is bleak. I, on the other hand, have a growing sense of doom.

Chapter 22

BEFORE AND AFTER

BY THE TIME WE REACH the library, our noses are red from the fog and wind. The relief we anticipated feeling inside is not to be, as we push through the doors to find that the heat is not working and it is just as cold inside as out. Miss Asher, wearing a blanket as a shawl, sits at her desk studying her computer screen. Please let it be work related and not dragon related.

"Heat is out," she says. But as soon as she glances up, she gasps, and I remember too late my bruised face. "Cassie, what happened to you?"

"Skateboarding accident," I say quickly. "Joe was teaching me." I elbow him hard.

"Right!" he blurts. "I tried to teach her a kiwi flip. Turns out she is really bad." He snickers.

"I hit the curb with my face," I say, piling on.

"Did you see a doctor?" Miss Asher comes from behind her desk to examine my face up close. "Is anything broken? Do you need an ice pack?" Jeez, it's not that bad. She's overreacting. I hold Albert extra tightly in his pouch. If he makes a break for it now, we are in trouble.

"Nothing broken," I say. "Just, you know, black and blue. I'm supposed to ice it, but I just go outside. It's Lewiston, after all. Ha ha. It doesn't even hurt. So no heat in the building today?"

"You don't have to stay," Miss Asher replies. "Making you shelve books in the Arctic seems inhumane, and you seem to have suffered enough in the last twenty-four hours." Well, she's got that part right, anyway.

"Oh, we don't care," I say quickly. "We're not sugar cubes."

Joe stares at me. "Sugar cubes?"

It is something my father used to tell me when I said I didn't want to do things, like walk in the rain or handle the worms in the garden. Sugar cubes melt. Humans don't. You will be fine. Although I don't think he'd like me applying the sentiment to taking something that doesn't belong to me.

You're borrowing it, Cassie! No big deal!

That's a stretch on the word "borrow," but I plan to have the notebook back in its drawer before anyone is the wiser. "Never mind about the sugar cubes," I say. "We should get to work. Those books won't shelve themselves!"

Joe grins widely. Now that I've known him for a little while, I know this to be a fake smile. He is psyching himself up to distract Miss Asher. "Miss Asher," he says, jumping right in. "I wanted to ask you about a networking preference in the computer room." He gestures for her to follow. "I think we can get more power out of the mesh network. But I have a few questions. Unless you are busy?"

"Not at all," she says, trailing after him, the blanket flowing behind her like a cape. My pulse quickens. This is it. I watch until they disappear around the corner, count to ten just to be sure they aren't coming back, and pounce on the drawer. Maybe it will be open. I pull. Nope. I hip check it. More nope. I brace my feet and yank. This doesn't work either. There's a jar of paper clips on the desk. Joe never got around to telling me *how*, exactly, the girl picked the lock in the video, but how hard can it be?

I dump out the jar of paper clips, looking for the fat ones. The contents spill across the desk. And there in the middle is a small key that looks suspiciously like the one that Miss Asher wears around her neck. Is it a duplicate? An extra? Can it be this easy? As I slide the key into the drawer lock and hear a satisfying click, I think about how maybe the universe does care about me, maybe just a tiny little bit.

Inside the drawer is the pale yellow notebook with the map symbol sketched on the cover. I stuff it under my hoodie just as Joe's voice floats toward me. He's speaking loudly, something about a malfunctioning portion of the network. Slamming the drawer shut, I lock it and shovel the clips and the key back into the jar, placing it back in its proper location and pivoting to the trolley cart of books I am meant to be shelving in one fluid movement that makes me think I might have superhero potential after all. I smile at Joe and Miss Asher.

"Did you get everything fixed?" I ask.

Joe makes a weird face. "Yes. *Did you?*"

I nod. Joe exhales. I invite him to help me with the book shelving. He agrees much too quickly, but the heating-repair people have arrived, and Miss Asher's attention has shifted. Grabbing the trolley, we rush to the safety and invisibility of the stacks. We hunker down on the floor, obscured by rows of medieval history books that no one ever reads. The notebook rests against my knees. Joe holds up his phone, showing the image from the closet door. The symbols are the *same*. We glance at each other, a feeling between us that we can't quite articulate, the sense that once we open this notebook things will be different. There will be a "before" and an "after."

I take a deep breath. Joe swallows a few times.

"Here goes," I say.

A few old newspaper clippings fall from between the covers like confetti. But Miss Asher has all those paper clips. Why not use them?

"Check this out." It's an article with a blurry photograph of a smiling Miss Asher from about six years ago. The caption reads *Young librarian takes helm at Lewiston library*.

"'Miss Asher,'" Joe reads aloud, "'a lifelong resident of Lewiston, is set to make big changes at the Lewiston library.' Starting with getting the heat to work."

"Do you think she always wanted to be a librarian?" I ask with wonder. I can't even guess what I'll be when I grow up. Besides, the future feels vague to me, unformed somehow, as if it could go in any direction and when it does it won't ask my permission.

"Look at this one." Joe hands me another clip. Miss Asher again, this time as a little kid, standing in front of the library holding a big trophy for winning her age group in a reading contest. Of *course* she did. So maybe she did always know she wanted to be a librarian.

Miss Asher's voice rings out through the stacks. "There's another trolley here, if you kids can stand the cold! I might make hot chocolate!"

"Still working on these!" I yell back. "Hot chocolate sounds great!"

"We have to hurry," Joe whispers, gathering up the news clippings and putting them aside. I flip to the first page of the notebook. Nothing special, a bit faded around the edges. The handwriting is in swirling purple ink with a lot of distracting flourishes. Definitely Miss Asher's penmanship. She likes to decorate her letters and words, like an illuminated manuscript from the Middle Ages.

"Read," Joe demands.

The first page is dated February 3, thirteen years ago. Great. It's a diary, and reading someone else's diary is about the worst thing you can do. "It's a diary," I say.

"No, it's not," Joe replies. "It's a research journal. It says so right on the cover."

That is like calling a duck a goose. I mean, the duck is *still* a duck, regardless of the label.

"It's from the year Miss Asher graduated from Lewiston Senior High School," Joe continues. "Which means this is probably from when she was seventeen. Hurry up. *Read*."

I clear my throat and begin.

Chapter 23

THE NOTEBOOK

Date: February 18

Time: 10:30 PM

Location: my bedroom

Do you know how I always complain that Lewiston is the most boring place on earth? And how I can't wait to go to college someplace interesting, where life is exciting all the time and things actually happen?

Well, something <u>finally</u> happened here. Sort of, anyway.

Mom volunteered me (so annoying) to help the town library move their archives to the university after the flood. Of course, I turned around and volunteered Shel, because why not? He's my best friend, and it's good for him to get out. With Cyrus being so sick, he gets antsy when he's at home too much. Anyway, not the point.

Old Mrs. Weber, the librarian who I swear walked with the dinosaurs, left us completely alone (I think she was napping at her desk), which means we were able to poke around in all of the stuff.

And there is a box labeled "Dragons." For real! Dragons! Well, Shel and I jumped right on that one, because . . . like . . . what? The first thing we pulled out was a flyer, the kind of old advertisement you'd tack up in the town square or something. It was two panels. The first showed a black-and-white sketch of a man clutching his head and his stomach, obviously ailing and not long for this world. And the second showed the same guy, but fully healed and enjoying a cup of tea, surrounded by his adoring family. In block letters across the top of the ad, it read:

Tenbrook Miracle Serum
Cure gout, toothaches, festering wounds, fever,
irritability of temper, fear, dread, insomnia,
melancholy, broken bones
The shop on Avid Street (third door on the right)
Post-free

Shel and I had a good laugh over the "irritability of temper" thing. But there was more in the archival dragon box: a deed to a grand mansion and other properties; invitations to society balls in faraway San Francisco; bills from dressmakers and milliners (those are old-timey hat makers, by the way). These Tenbrooks were loaded! They had milliners! Ha ha. Bad pun I know, but still, can't help myself.

There was also a fat pile of faded forest scene sketches. The artist must have been doing a study of a particular grove of trees, because they covered it from about fifty different perspectives, including a bunch of close-ups, too. Shel and I thought the artist deserved an A+ because they were pretty amazing, almost like black-and-white photographs.

At the bottom of the box we discovered a journal belonging to some guy named Edward Tenbrook. It was not in great shape, but we got the basics of his tale. And let me tell you, it's a whopper! I just <u>have</u> to write it down! If I ever become a famous author (maybe?), it might make the basis of a good book.

Edward, twelve years old, was dirt poor, the youngest of eight kids. He was pretty much hungry, cold, and miserable all the time. Walking among the tall trees (I assume Arcata wilderness?) was the only thing that brought him happiness. The trees would have come right to the edge of town back then, before they logged them halfway to extinction. But then one day, out in the forest, Edward meets a dragon. Not. Kidding. A dragon.

Her name was Alvina, and she had run away from her tyrannical father, Vayne, who happened to be king of dragons and pretty awful. Her family belonged to the dragon ruling class, the Silvers. The Silvers held all the power and wealth. Silvers were well fed and content while others went hungry. Alvina said there was plenty for everyone, but the Silvers kept everything for themselves, as they had for centuries. Their grip was unbreakable.

See what I mean about this making a great book?! And I'm not even to the good part yet. There was a prophecy, a prediction about the future made by a revered elder, who claimed a dragon would rise to overthrow the ruling Silvers, ending their reign. This dragon would travel great distances and overcome many challenges. And he would bear a special mark. Fearful of losing his power, Vayne ordered all marked dragons be executed.

Obviously Alvina was pretty horrified by that proclamation. She tried to intervene, but Vayne grew furious, and, in fear, Alvina fled through a rip between dimensions. The rip was like a wormhole and served as a gateway between the dragon world and our world, a rip we humans did not even know was there. Which is probably good. Wherever we go, we seem to mess things up.

Okay. Where was I? Alvina the dragon came through the rip. Now, she knew about the rip only because she had learned of it from her grandmother, who was not meant to share that information. Keeping dragons from knowing of the rips was another way for Vayne to keep control, because the dragons would certainly leave if they could, right?

I have to say I'm dazzled by Edward's ability to tie it all together so it almost feels . . . <u>believable</u>. Okay. Let's keep going. Shel says I get easily sidetracked, and I don't want to do that now. This story is just too good!

When Alvina came through the rip, the weather went insane, you know, violent bizarre storms, like the very boundaries of reality were being shredded, which, in a way, I guess they were. Edward and Alvina become best buddies (Shel

said just like us!). But they could only spend
a handful of hours together because I guess
being here in our dimension was hard on
Alvina. It made her weak. And then she would
have to leave. But even a few hours made
Edward the happiest kid on the planet. He
finally had a friend, his first one. Edward was
so taken with his new and only friend that he
wandered around daydreaming and got himself
run over by a horse and cart.

It was bad. His leg got infected, and antibiotics
weren't invented until 1928! Things were
looking grim.

And this is where our storyteller Edward really
cranks it up a notch. Check this out: Alvina
<u>cured</u> Edward. Like, <u>all better</u>, don't die of
gangrene or lose your leg or any of the many
terrible ways this could have turned out. Nope.
Turns out dragon blood can work miracles
on the human body. However, Alvina did so
at great risk to herself, because being here
already made her weak, and sharing her blood

just made it worse. Alvina was a mess. Edward, back on his feet quite literally, was in a race against time to get her through the rip and save her life. But how to find the rip? He had no idea where it was other than somewhere in the woods. And Lewiston has a lot of woods.

But he had to try! Unfortunately, Edward's scheming, nasty, desperate family found them. Instead of marveling at the existence of dragons and the miracle of Edward's recovery, they kidnapped Alvina!

You read that right! They took her prisoner and stole her blood for, you guessed it, the Tenbrook Magical Serum. Edward tried to save his friend, but they just locked him up in a freezing-cold cabin in the woods, where his awful brothers occasionally threw moldy crusts of bread at him. So not okay.

But wait, the story is not over! Upon discovering Alvina's imprisonment, Vayne came through the rip to save her. He was dreadful, yes, but she was still his daughter and heir to the dragon throne. But he arrived too late, and, finding her already dead, he laid waste to the Tenbrook family in revenge. He burned it <u>all</u>.

So the Great Lewiston Fire of 1850 that they forced us to learn all about in school? That wasn't lightning. It was a dragon.
As for what happened next, we have to wait, because the diary was disintegrating in my hands, and old Mrs. Weber insisted the entire box be turned over to the university for restoration. I know! It makes me want to scream. I hate waiting.

In the meantime, Shel and I agreed to track down everything we can on this whole dragons/rips/revenge thing. He seemed really into it, about as happy and awake as he has been since Cyrus got sick, so even though I know this whole story isn't true and is probably the result of Edward hitting his head or something, I'm going with it.

I know Shel worries about his brother all the time, and I wish I could say something to help. But I know how he will respond—he will tell me I don't have a twin, so I can't possibly understand that anything that happens to Cyrus feels like it is happening to him. Like, for real happening. So I just don't say anything.

Date: March 15
Time: 11:13 PM
Location: living room couch/TV is on. So annoying.
Here's something weird. When we went to check with the university archives to see when Edward's diary would be finished, they had no idea what we were talking about! There was no record of it. Sure, there was the box with the papers and flyers and letters and junk, but no diary. Even when I told them I was the one who had dropped it off with their restoration department. They just shrugged and looked sheepish and embarrassed. But, you know, I couldn't help but think that they were lying, that something else was going on. It felt off.

Meanwhile, Shel is kinda getting . . . obsessed. He is sure if we can find one of Edward's dragons, he can take their blood and save Cyrus. Warning alarms went off in my head when he said this. I figured we were just having some fun, but now Shel spends every minute in the university library researching. He's identifying locations where extreme weather has happened and then searching for rumors of dragon sightings. He swears he can create a map to the rips and find a dragon. He says he will go through and take one if he has to! He's writing to weather experts all over the world now! I'm worried what they will think. Because I know what it makes me think.

Date: April 26
Time: midnight
Location: under my covers
I can't sleep. I finally told Shel that I thought all this Alvina/Edward stuff is made up. There are no dragons. There is no magic serum. He can't save Cyrus. He is taking it all much too

seriously. I mean, he's not even going to school. He's about to fail chemistry!

And then I said that even if there was a dragon, kidnapping them, keeping them here, and stealing their blood would kill them. Look what happened to Alvina! And who are we to say one life is more valuable than another? Why do we get to decide?

Well. That did not go over well. Shel FLIPPED out. He raged at me. He told me I didn't understand what it was like to watch his brother shrink down to a skeleton, too weak to even feed himself or laugh anymore. I tried to tell him I am here for him in whatever way he needs, but he was just in a fury, yelling that the dragon we need could be here right now. Metallic dragons shape-shift, he said. They could be among us.

I had never seen Shel like that. His eyes were frantic, like the Shel I've always known was not even there anymore. I got scared and left.

I don't know if we are friends anymore.

Date: May 5

Time: 6:00 PM

Location: front porch

Remember I said that Lewiston was boring? Well, I take that back! Weirdness is everywhere. Today on my way home from school I was stopped by a man and a lady. Black suits. Sunglasses (in Lewiston? Duh?). Badges. The man was kind of old, gray hair, wrinkles, but the lady didn't look that much older than me! They claimed to be some subdivision of the FBI, like cold cases involving unlikely phenomena? Or something? Whatever that even means! Anyway, the identification appeared to be real, so I agreed to talk to them but only on the sidewalk in full view of the people at the pizza place across the street. Smart, right?

But guess what they asked about? Edward Tenbrook's diary! I swear to you! WHAT is going on? I answered their questions as best I could and then told them the diary was gone, which did not surprise them, so I guess they checked the archives, too. They asked me who else knew about the diary, and for some reason—let's call it

instinct—I lied and said no one. I did not mention
Shel. If FBI agents showed up on his doorstep and
he started telling them all sorts of stuff about his
dragon-hunting brigade, they might lock him up
and throw away the key.

Anyway, they left me their cards. Agent Hillsdale
is the old guy. Agent Fox is the young one.

My first thought was to run directly to Shel's house
and tell him about the agents.

But then I remembered we aren't friends anymore.

Date: June 25
Time: after dinner
Location: the roof

Cyrus died this morning. Mom said she thought
Shel would appreciate a visit, but she doesn't
understand. He hates me. He thinks if I had
helped him, if I had believed in him like friends
are supposed to, we might have been able to
find a dragon and save his brother.

But how can he blame me for not finding what
isn't there?

Chapter 24

A CAT ON THE LOOSE

I CAN HEAR JOE'S rapid breathing in my ear as we stare at the notebook page. But we don't have time to freak out. Miss Asher's footsteps echo on the tile. She is coming to see why we have disappeared. Just in time, I scoop up a pile of books and hide the diary underneath them. Miss Asher appears, blanket lofting behind her.

"Do you hear that?" she asks, holding a cupped hand to her ear for emphasis. Somewhere in this cavernous building, the ancient heating units have struggled to life, rumbling like grumpy giants. A tendril of warmth drifts down from a ceiling vent. "A thing of wonder, even if we can't see it. Come on, I have hot chocolate and doughnuts. You guys have gone above and beyond today."

As we trail behind Miss Asher, Joe grips my arm. "There is a ninety percent chance my head will explode," he says casually. I completely understand. How to absorb it all? At least we know Albert came here through a rip from another dimension, and that's why the weather has been out of control. But is being here hurting him? Is Albert safe as long as he remains a kitten? In the journal, Shel says metallic dragons can shape-shift. Even so, Albert is not metallic, so what does it mean that he can turn himself into a cat? I have a lot of questions, all of them urgent.

And that's not even including how Shel and Miss Asher were best friends and Shel is almost certainly puffy-orange-jacket Sheldon Slack. He wanted to hunt dragons and save his twin brother's life, but Miss Asher didn't believe that dragons were real. She thought Edward Tenbrook was a great storyteller, a fiction writer, someone who made up the whole thing.

With the heat issue resolved, a steady stream of patrons fills the library. Miss Asher greets each one like an old friend. She reminds them the library closes early today because it is Saturday. She makes book recommendations.

She chats about pets and children and the bizarre weather. Joe and I stuff our faces with doughnuts and drink hot chocolate, because if we don't, Miss Asher will definitely know something is up.

But all I can think about is reading the next section of her journal, the unanswered questions gathering strength like a thundercloud in my head. Fortunately, old Ms. Martinez has cornered Miss Asher. She likes to talk about gardening and can do so all day if given the opportunity. Joe nudges me and gestures toward the old fiction section. Everyone wants to read the new stuff, which is out front, not the old stuff, which is back in a dark corner on dusty shelves. We should be safe in the old fiction section, and unseen.

Except a bald man wanders into our section. We act supremely interested in a collection of Stephen King novels as he passes by. He doesn't even notice us, and quickly rounds the corner to the authors whose last names start with *L*. This is good, because in my pocket, Albert stretches and grumbles. A second later his head pops out and he surveys the scene. Not familiar. No food bowl. This is a problem. He meows so loudly, the bald man reappears around the back end of the shelving unit, blinking rapidly.

"Did I hear a . . . cat?" he asks. Joe looks at me, panicked.

"Ah . . . no?" I reply, stuffing Albert back in my pocket, which he does not like. "No cats here. It's a library. Lots of books about cats, but no actual cats."

"I *heard* a cat," the man mutters to himself. "I *know* I heard a cat." But he disappears again without further questioning.

I turn my back and pull Albert out of my pocket, and we get face-to-face. "You need to be quiet."

His response is even louder. How can something so small make so much noise? The bald man flies back into view. "There is definitely a cat! I'm terribly allergic. I'm getting the librarian!"

"It's not real!" Joe shouts. "It's just this app." He holds up his phone, and a mechanical, electronic meow blasts forth. In my pocket, Albert goes stiff.

"That's *not* what it sounded like," the man protests.

"But that's what you heard," I say. "Because there are no cats in the library."

He doesn't believe us. The fake cat does not sound like the real one at all. But we have undermined his confidence, making him doubt himself, so he backs away, out of sorts, without another word.

"Albert is getting restless," I whisper to Joe. "We have to get out of here."

"Do we take the notebook?" Joe asks. "Do we put it back?"

But as it turns out, we don't even have long enough to answer those basic questions.

Albert has reached his threshold for captivity and oddball cat sounds. He leaps from my pocket in a mad dash for freedom, flying through the air and landing right at the feet of the bald man, who yells out, triumphant, "See? I *knew* there was a cat!"

It is pandemonium, and not in a good, fun way.

Albert zooms around the man and disappears into the stacks. I race after him. Joe races after me. As I skid around the far end of the fiction shelves, almost plowing into a trolley of books, the notebook flies out of my hands. But I can't lose sight of Albert. If I do, it is game over.

"Albert, come back right now!" I hiss. Even though I brought a cat in here, I feel I should still try to respect the rules of the library and not bellow like a water buffalo. Joe feels no such compunction.

"Grab him, Cassie!" he shouts. "He's right there!"

"Both of you stop right now!" Miss Asher yells. She appears with her hands on her hips, scowling. Oh boy. Now we've done it. But we can't exactly stop. Albert skirts under the lowest metal shelf. I cut around the far side, hoping to head him off. But he's wise to my plan and takes off in the opposite direction. Cats, in case you were wondering, are *not* obedient. They don't sit or roll over or fetch or come when you call them. How come it wasn't a cute little abandoned puppy in that dumpster, who wanted nothing more than to please me?

I catch a black blur at the end of the aisle and run toward it. Just as Albert tries to bolt from under the shelves, I throw myself like a baseball player sliding into home, catching just the end of his tail. He howls in protest and swats at my hand. I refuse to let go despite the tiny daggers digging into my skin. You'd think he'd be nicer after I saved his life and all. I get my other hand around his small round belly and drag him toward me. His eyes glow a fierce red, and, surprised, I almost let go. A startling crack of thunder shakes the library.

At Mia's house, when Albert turned into a dragon, he was protecting me. But what if he turns into a dragon because he's *mad* at me?

That would not be good. In fact, that would be all kinds of bad. I hold him tight. "I love you," I whisper, "but you are being very naughty, and we are going to get into serious trouble. It's time to shape up." The red in his eyes fades, and his whiskers twitch. He licks a paw and casually drags it over his face, his way of saying he allowed himself to be caught, that it was all planned. Cats do not like to be embarrassed. It is only when I sit up that I realize Miss Asher stands over us, her face as pale as the moon.

"His eyes," she whispers, almost to herself. "Were his eyes really . . . glowing?"

I pull Albert closer to me. I should have just run away. Coming here was a bad idea. Joe stands just beyond her left shoulder, wringing his hands. He knows this was a bad idea too. Miss Asher squats down beside me and runs a hand over Albert's head. He arches into the touch and purrs. Traitor. "The golden blaze," she mutters to herself, eyes intensely focused on Albert. "Can it all be true? Was I wrong?"

She is about to reach out and take him from me when a loud pinging noise erupts throughout the library. It's the cell phones, all going off at once. Miss Asher points a finger in my face. "Stay here. Don't move. I will be right back."

Joe pulls out his phone, and his face contorts. "Oh boy. Things just got urgent. We need to get out of here. Now!" He shoves me toward the rear exit. It's a fire door. If we open it, an alarm will go off. Aren't we in enough trouble?

"Joe, the alarm!"

"Hasn't worked in years," he says, plowing through the door without a second thought.

And we run.

Chapter 25

A DANGEROUS GIRL

OUR OVERLOADED BACKPACKS bounce hard against our spines. Sweat blooms on my forehead despite the cold. Joe does not slow down enough for me to ask what happened. We dodge between cars and across streets. It feels like random zigzags. Does Joe have a plan, a destination? Near City Hall, we are consumed by the weekend farmers market crowd, moving slowly among tables stacked high with fresh kale, apples, and bunches of carrots. There's a five-person band playing country music under a covered gazebo, a dozen food trucks, a coffee kiosk, and several vendors offering baked goods that make my stomach growl despite the many doughnuts I've eaten. The Lewiston farmers market is the hot ticket on Saturday morning. I don't understand why adults get so excited about a bunch of vegetables, but nobody asked me.

"Hurry up," Joe urges. He darts away from the market, onto a side street of three-story apartment buildings. I follow closely at his heels. We veer into an alley between buildings, and Joe stops abruptly, leaning up against the wall and gasping. "The phones all going off," he wheezes. "It's an alert from the Lewiston police. For *you*."

He holds out his phone. My face, from a sixth-grade school photo, fills the screen. What the heck? The Lewiston police use the community's network of cell phones to alert the citizens if something important is happening, like a forest fire to be avoided or a car crash that is messing up traffic.

Or if there is a dangerous criminal on the loose.

The alert includes a description of my hoodie. It says I am potentially harboring a dangerous animal and should be approached with caution. They are careful not to specify what *kind* of dangerous animal I happen to be harboring. If the Wilsons reported that a dragon was in their daughter's bedroom and may have singed the hair of one of her friends, the police would have raised an eyebrow. No way they were buying that. They probably think I have a secret pet mountain lion or eagle or something else wild but not something *imaginary*. None of this changes the fact that the police are after me. Miss Asher always says that it is better to lead with curiosity when approaching the unknown. Putting fear forward can end in trouble. But right now I'm scared, for me and for Albert.

Detective Rhodes must have figured out I was not my mother on the phone. Or she finally picked up when the Wilsons called. Or any number of possibilities I just didn't consider. I should have left last night. I should have gone while I had the chance. I rest a hand on Albert, who seems to have a knack for sleeping through the exciting parts.

"If we can make it to the train station," Joe says, "we can get out of here. I give us a seventy-five percent chance of success." He shrugs off his backpack and digs around inside, producing a spare baseball hat and a blue rain jacket. He sure is better prepared for running away than I am. "You'll have to go incognito. Turn your sweatshirt inside out and put this over it. And the hat."

I put on the jacket and the hat. To get to the train station, we have to skirt around the edge of the farmers market crowd. Despite being incognito, I'm sure everyone is looking at me, the wanted girl harboring the dangerous unknown animal. "Joe. Everyone is staring."

"No they aren't," he says too quickly. "They are buying celery or whatever. Keep walking. Maybe look down. Okay, some of them might have noticed you. We should move faster."

Joe slices through the crowd, elbowing around tight groups to find channels of space, looking for a way out. Do police alerts come with rewards? Is there a bounty on my head? People study their phones and me and their phones again. They know. They *all* know. A few of them move toward us.

"Joe."

"Cassie."

"We are in serious trouble."

"I know."

"What do we do?"

"Run?"

"Again?"

"Do you have a better idea?"

"No."

"Ready?"

"Yup."

"Let's do this."

We bolt. Not subtle but necessary. The crowd is like an undulating wave of bodies. Maneuvering as best we can, I keep glancing over my shoulder to see if anyone is actively following, but I can't tell. I keep a firm grip on Albert. If he jumps out, he will be trampled, or worse.

"Quick! This way!" There is a food truck taking advantage of the gathering, a big line snaking from the order window. Several large plastic garbage bins are lined up behind the truck. We duck behind them. A few suspicious people pause in front of the food truck. They look this way and that, maybe searching for us, but we are nowhere to be seen. After a few long moments, they trudge off, swallowed by the crowd.

I relax my shoulders, which have migrated up to my ears. "They're gone," I say.

"That was close." Joe squats next to me on the dirty pavement, wiping the sweat from his forehead. "I had no idea that this adventure was going to be so intense."

"You can go home," I say quickly. "I mean, you don't have to do this." I mean, I'm wanted by the *police*. I'm pretty sure Joe helping me escape is against the law.

Joe stares at me, eyes wide. "Are you kidding me? This is the most fun I've had maybe ever in my life. No way I'm leaving. We are on a mysterious quest for answers, fraught with danger. It's almost like we are pirates. It's pretty excellent."

My cheeks grow warm at his words. But instead of telling him they mean a lot to me, I just mutter that we should get moving before we are noticed. The alley behind the food truck leads to another narrow street lined with small cottages. This street takes us right up behind the train station. It's empty back here, just dumpsters and some discarded boxes, a perfect place to hide until the train arrives.

Sitting on some abandoned plastic bins, I pull a snoozing Albert from my pocket. "How do you manage to sleep through all this?" I ask him. I mean, I know cats sleep seventeen hours a day, but this seems remarkable anyway. Albert opens half an eye and, not seeing anything worth eating, closes it again. Oh well. Joe paces in front of me. It is the first time we can actually talk about what we read in Miss Asher's notebook. I don't even know where to start.

"I'm thinking something," Joe says.

I'm glad someone is. My brain feels like it is close to short-circuiting. Joe settles down beside me on the plastic bins and pulls out his phone. After a few taps, the 3D map appears on the small screen.

"Edward Tenbrook lived in Lewiston," he says, indicating the line ending in the Arcata wilderness, just north of Lewiston. "And in his diary, he claimed he met a dragon in the woods."

"Okay," I say. "And?"

"What if this is a map to the *rips*? The places where dragons can come and go? I mean, we didn't find a description of the symbol in the notebook or why it was on the cover, but I think I'm right."

Oh wow. This feels big. "We know of two dragons," I say quickly. "Alvina, who was Edward's friend. And Albert. Both found here."

"Exactly!"

"And I bet if we did the research, we'd find stories in these places." I gesture to the lines leading to Japan, London, Greece, Botswana, and the other locations.

"I bet Slack already *did*," Joe replies. "Remember the boxes of research from his video? Who knows what he knows?"

"A rip in the Arcata woods," I whisper. Joe is right. I can feel it in my bones. But before I get to say so, there is a noise that grabs my attention.

A person watching us. In a puffy orange jacket.

Chapter 26

PUT TWO AND TWO TOGETHER, AND WHAT DO YOU GET? A DRAGON.

SHELDON SLACK IS RIGHT HERE behind the train station, among the smelly dumpsters and recycling. He steps forward. The shirt under his jacket is wrinkled with what looks to be coffee stains down the front. His eyes are wild, like he hasn't slept in a very long time. I feel a mix of fear and pity.

"What do you want?" I croak.

He grins, showing off those vampire teeth, and fear definitely edges out pity. There are no such things as vampires, but there are no such things as dragons, either, and look how that turned out.

"The weather, the video, the police alert," Slack says,

his eyes darting every which way. "If you put two and two together, why, I might go so far as to suggest the dangerous animal you are harboring is a dragon. And I *want* that dragon. *Where* is he?"

Joe moves in right behind me and clutches the back of my hoodie. I don't have to look at him to know he is scared.

"I won't turn you in," Slack continues. "Just give him to me."

Sometimes the best thing a girl without a plan can do is stall. "Why do you want him?" I ask.

"I want the *power* to save people," Slack says, eyes narrowed, lips pressed into a tight thin line. "I want to be the one who takes away the pain of loss." I remember what Miss Asher said to Sheldon Slack in the library, that he'd completely scrambled the means and the ends. He may have started out wanting to save people from suffering, but now it's about the power.

Knowing this, however, does not help. We are still trapped. Slack blocks our only escape route. He moves closer. "Where is the dragon?" he hisses. "Just tell me and no one gets hurt."

"No one but the dragon, you mean," I whisper.

"What did you just say?" He is so close now, I can see the sweat gathered on his forehead. My heart pounds, and

Albert must know I'm scared, because from my hoodie pocket comes a deep guttural growl. His little body goes tense. Slack points a finger at me. "Are you cooperating or *not*?"

My pocket growls again. "Not," I reply. And with that, Albert, wiggling loose from my grip, explodes from his hideout, a tiny furious fuzz ball. Paws planted on the ground, he crouches low, ears flat, prepared to attack. Being he's the size of a cantaloupe, it's hardly intimidating. Brows furrowed in confusion, Slack considers him. "What is going on?" He makes a face. "I hate cats. Awful creatures."

"Oh," I whisper, "you shouldn't have said that."

A sudden, sharp clap of thunder rings out, and the air fills with electricity and thick smoke. "What the . . ." Slack coughs and gags, waving at the air in front of him and stepping away from me. Joe clutches my sweatshirt hard enough to strangle me. But I stand firm, feet planted, a weird sort of pride filling my chest.

"Cassie, what is happening?" Joe cries.

From the cloud emerges a dragon. Albert.

His eyes blaze red hot and fierce, his leathery lips are pulled back, revealing a row of jagged teeth. The golden blaze glows like flame, and his wings pulse with power.

"Cassie!" Joe shouts. "He's a *dragon*!"

"I told you he was," I reply. Joe clings to me like lint.

"I don't think I really believed it until right now."

Slack came here hunting dragons, and yet there he stands, trembling with fear, his eyes as wide as saucers. I get it. I really do. It's a shock no matter what you believe. No one moves.

Albert gets very close to Slack. Flames jump from his nostrils. Slack quivers and shakes. "He's *real*," he whispers. In response, Albert growls, coiling his tail and swinging it through the air like an out-of-control fire hose.

"You should go," I say.

Slack nods, dumbfounded, all plans of kidnapping a dragon temporarily swallowed up by his shock. "I should go," he repeats. "I am going." Slowly, he backs down the alley, tripping over some cardboard boxes and disappearing around the corner.

"I warned him," I mutter.

Albert watches until Slack is well and truly gone and then turns his attention to us. Stepping forward, he growls low and sniffs the air. He paws the ground. His face is right next to mine now. I can smell his hot breath and see the serrated edges of his long teeth. Slowly, the blazing red in his eyes fades, replaced by mossy green. Albert's eyes. He nudges me, forehead to shoulder. I place my hands on either side of his head.

And suddenly the silver dragon from my dream is back in my thoughts, as if Albert put her there directly. *Home.* I know Albert is not safe here, not from Sheldon Slack, or the Lewiston police, or, possibly, some weird division of the FBI. Just being in our dimension hurts him. I cannot keep him here just because I love him. This idea is so powerful and unwelcome that I barely notice Joe, cowering, still clutching a handful of my hoodie.

"Okay, so this is really happening," Joe whispers. "Of course, it's not as if a unicorn fell out of the sky or anything. I mean, a unicorn would be *really* weird. Like, I'm not sure I could handle a unicorn. But a cat that transforms into a dragon? Sure thing. No big deal. Oh man, I feel a little light-headed." Joe erupts in a burst of hysterical laughter followed closely by hyperventilation. Gasping, he flails around like a baby bird kicked out of the nest.

I grab him by the shoulders. "Take a deep breath," I command, "and put your arms above your head." He nods frantically but can't seem to get his arms in the air. "Look at me. Like this." I pull one up and then the other. "Like tree pose in that stupid yoga they make us do in PE class. Make like a tree." He continues to nod as his arms wobble beside his ears. "Perfect. Nice tree. You got this. You're fine. Nothing is going to happen. I promise. You can trust me."

I don't know if any of this is true except for the part about his tree being pretty good. Joe's breathing slows. His eyes stop pinwheeling in his head. "Okay? Good? Keep breathing. Just like that. Perfect."

Keeping a hand on Joe, just in case he suddenly collapses, I slowly turn back toward Albert, only to find the dragon is gone and the kitten has returned, a tiny ball asleep on the alley pavement. I elbow Joe and point. "Look."

Joe cocks his head to the left. I can't tell if he is going to laugh or cry. "My arms are tired," he says after a pause. "Can I put them down?"

I nod. "Yeah. And how about we get out of here before anything else extraordinary happens? Like unicorns falling from the sky or something." I giggle. I can't help it.

Joe squints at me. "You just had to, didn't you?"

"I did." Real laughter starts to bubble up. Tears pool in my eyes. Before I know it, I'm doubled over, gasping.

"I don't particularly like unicorns!" Joe yells. "I'm sorry that everyone is obsessed with them, but I think they are strange."

"And cat-dragons aren't?" I squeak.

"I didn't say that. Get it together, Cassie. We need a place where no one will find us so we can figure out what to do. The train is right out of the question." Uh-oh. This is funny too. Tears roll down my cheeks.

Joe throws his arms up in the air. "I give up!"

I try to stand. He's right. We need to get out of here, like, right away. Deep breaths. No laughing.

"Okay. Okay. The botanical gardens. I know a place in there where we can get lost."

Scooping up the sleeping kitten, I stuff him into my pocket, throw Joe his backpack, and shrug into mine. "Let's go," I say.

"That's what I've been saying," Joe replies, exasperated. "And for the record, I have no problem with rainbows."

"Who said anything about rainbows?"

"They are often associated with unicorns," Joe says.

I feel the edges of my lips tug up. If he says "unicorns" or "rainbows" one more time, I cannot be responsible for my actions. At a swift pace, we exit the alley and cut across a small park, heading for the gardens. It feels almost normal, like we are just two kids hanging out on a Saturday afternoon.

Except for the dragon in my pocket.

Chapter 27

THE BOTANICAL GARDEN

WE STICK TO THE SIDE STREETS, careful to avoid any other people or incidents. My stomach churns with left-over adrenaline from the Slack encounter.

He's not safe here.

I know that!

Suddenly dizzy, I stop in the middle of the sidewalk and bend over, hands on knees, lungs constricted. "Cassie!" Joe stands before me, hands on hips. "Come on! We can't stop. What's wrong with you?"

"I might puke," I say weakly.

"Are you sick?"

"No . . . just . . . everything."

Joe pats me on the back. "You can puke in the gardens when we are out of sight. Now come *on*. Get moving." You'd never know that mere moments ago I had to put him in tree pose so he didn't faint.

I shake my spinning head and follow closely at Joe's heels, concentrating on his footfalls as my stomach threatens to erupt. One step and another and another, and before too long we disappear into the Lewiston Memorial Garden, a series of intricate garden beds surrounded by winding paths, lined with delicate maples and robust cherry trees. At this time of year, the late-fall blooms are a riot of orange and red and yellow. In the farthest garden corner are two benches, hidden inside an elaborate circle of sharp winterberry holly shrubs. Once inside the circle, the muffled silence is complete. There is a hint of root beer wafting on the air from a bed of white rhododendrons nearby. As we enter the circle, Joe lets go a low whistle of appreciation.

"How did you find this place?" he asks.

"After my dad died," I say. "Sometimes the noise in my head just got really loud, and being here made it be quiet. If that makes any sense." I've never told anyone this, and instead of feeling anxious about revealing some small private part of myself to Joe, I'm relieved.

Joe nods. "I get that. Sometimes I lock myself in the bathroom to get away from my brothers. But this is nicer." He sits down with a heavy sigh, eyeing me from under the stiff brim of his ball cap.

"It did happen, didn't it?" he asks slowly.

I sit down beside him. "What?"

"You *know*," he says. "Everything?"

I get what he's asking. "It did," I say. "All of it."

We sit with that for a long moment. When everything you thought was true no longer is, it's fine to take a few extra minutes to think it over. Finally Joe says, "Okay, I need a snack."

Diving headlong into his backpack, he comes out with granola bars, red apples, and fruit leather. Is this some sort of magical bottomless backpack that he failed to tell me about? Are we good enough friends now that he'd trust me with that information? I should think so. "In my house," Joe explains, "my brothers take all the good snacks before I even get a chance at them. And I end up with healthy stuff. Yuck."

He tosses me a granola bar that lands in my lap, right on Albert's head. The kitten grumbles and pops out of his pocket. I swear he has bags under his eyes. Can that happen to cats? He crawls out of my pocket, sniffing the granola bar and eyeing me suspiciously. I scoop out a handful of kibble from my stash and pile it on the bench right beside me. Never one to let a crisis get in the way of a meal, Albert happily jumps from my lap and begins raucously eating. Bits of cat food fly in every direction. Elegant he is *not*.

Eyes locked on Albert, Joe says, "I have a lot of questions. I'm not used to having so many questions. I'm the kind of kid who knows things, you know?"

I nod, even though I'm the kind of kid who doesn't know things in the first place. After Albert scarfs his last piece of cat food, he vigorously cleans his whiskers by licking his paw and running it over his face, again and again. He cannot be bothered to clean any other parts, but he is persnickety about his whiskers.

"Why do you think he's here?" Joe asks.

"I think he's *lost*," I say. "I think he fell through that rip by accident. I think he shape-shifted into a cat because . . . well . . . people don't like what they don't understand. I think there are dragons on the other side searching for him."

"That's . . . not what I expected you to say."

I tell him about the dream. I describe how the silver dragon was so desperate and grateful when she saw him and how he went right to her. And how there was joy in the air. I could feel it. "And when I asked him if he wanted to go home, he said yes. Although that might have been part of the dream. I don't know, really."

From down on the ground, Albert stares at us, listening. Joe places his hand on my shoulder. "Cassie, do we need to help him get *back*?" Albert jumps into my lap, eyes locked with mine, waiting for an answer.

I *know* the answer is yes. I just don't want to say it out loud because then it will be real, and I can already feel my heart splintering at his loss. I love him so much, and that is the reason I have to help him. Of course, I start to cry, and Joe freaks out.

"Here," he says, rooting around in his backpack, "you can have the rest of the fruit leather. Oh jeez."

"Thank you," I blubber. "I mean, I'm sorry I just . . . well . . . you know." And Joe lets me cry, because a good friend never tries to talk you out of your feelings, even if they wig him out. After a few minutes, I wipe my nose on my sleeve. "Okay. I'm done."

"Are you sure?" Joe asks, peering suspiciously at my face.

"Yes," I say briskly, back to business. "We need to find the rip and get Albert home before anything bad happens to him. Where do we start?"

"I've been thinking," Joe says quickly, glad to be over the crying part. He pulls the globe map back up on his phone, zooming in on the line leading to the Arcata wilderness. "Arcata is a million acres of woods at least, and it's not like we have coordinates or anything. What we have is this imprecise line. So how do we find the rip? It's like a needle in a haystack but worse. We don't even know what a rip in the fabric of space-time continuity or whatever looks like." He pauses. "There's a sentence I never thought I'd say, although it's pretty wild now that I did. Where's the notebook? I think it's our best bet for more details."

That moment in the library comes back to me when I had to decide to pick up the notebook or grab Albert. I went for the cat. "I don't have it," I confess. "I dropped it when I was trying to catch Albert."

"Okay, that's bad." Joe drums his fingers on the bench. "But remember that part she wrote about turning over the dragon box to the university for preservation?"

"Yeah, but Edward's journal mysteriously disappeared."

"I know, but I'm thinking about those sketches of woods that Miss Asher wrote about, where she said the artist should have won an award or something for his study of those trees."

"Oh, you think Edward was drawing *clues* to the rip locations?" I ask. "Like he figured out part of the puzzle but not the whole thing?"

"Exactly! Remember, we have a map. We know it's in those woods somewhere. Those sketches might help us pinpoint the location. We need to see if they are still in that box at the university library."

This is a good idea. A brilliant idea, actually. "Do you think they are still there? Will they let us in to look at them if we ask nicely?"

Joe doesn't answer my question. Instead he stares at Albert, who is chasing the dried leaves blowing in the breeze. "How do you think we can get him to turn into a dragon, other than, you know, being threatened by bullies?"

"For real?"

"Totally. If we are going to get into the university library, we might need help."

"I think that is a very bad plan." Asking politely is one thing. Asking politely with a dragon is another thing entirely.

"That makes it a perfect fit with the rest of our day."

Okay. Joe does have a point. I interrupt Albert's game of chase, which displeases him greatly, and hold him right up to my face.

"Albert." I use a stern serious voice. "Can you turn into a dragon whenever you want?"

"Not like *that*," Joe says, rolling his eyes. "He can't speak! Just tell him to turn into a dragon."

"Like, right *now*? *Here*?"

Joe nods. "I know you're worried being a dragon makes him weak like Alvina, but this is part of getting him home. We *need* him."

"Okay, okay," I say. "I get it. Albert, can you please turn into a dragon?" I quickly place him on the ground in case he does, but he just wiggles with delight and resumes his game of chasing the leaves. No dragons anywhere.

"That's a fail," Joe says, shoulders sagging.

"Maybe he just doesn't feel like it," I suggest.

Joe slumps on the bench, deflated. "Maybe he's just ordinary."

Albert suddenly reverses course and attacks Joe's shoelaces, hissing and baring his tiny fangs. Joe giggles. Albert digs and bites until he gets a lace free and proceeds to shred it with his needlelike claws.

"I don't think he liked you calling him ordinary," I say, laughing.

"So *can* he understand us?"

I don't know. When I called for him from Mia's bedroom,

I swear he heard me. And then he came. When I asked him if he wanted to go home, he said he did. I close my eyes.

"What are you doing?" Joe asks.

I hold up a hand for him to be quiet. Concentrating, I repeat to myself, *Albert, become a dragon* over and over like a mantra.

Albert, become a dragon.

Chapter 28

ALL IN MY HEAD

I DON'T KNOW HOW many times I say it, but it must be a lot. My trance is broken by a loud crack of thunder and smoke billowing in the air, just like before. And Albert emerges. I don't think this is ever going to get old. Quickly, I cover the short distance between us and throw my arms around him. He rumbles, a deep guttural sound that vibrates through my body. My dragon is purring!

I take his head in my hands and stare into his glittering emerald eyes. "I love you, Albert," I say. "I don't care what shape or size or . . . you know . . . it doesn't matter."

Albert gently pushes his forehead to mine. His skin is

warm and soft. The moment is interrupted by Joe tugging at my sleeve.

"*How* did you do that?" Joe demands, attention fixed on Albert. If Albert makes any sudden moves, Joe will surely jump right out of his skin.

"I don't know," I explain. "I just kind of asked in my head."

Joe takes a step closer to Albert. "So you talk to him in your head?"

"I wouldn't call it talking, exactly. And maybe it's just a coincidence. I don't know. It's hard to explain."

Joe takes another step closer to Albert. "Coincidence is at least ten percent better than nothing." He reaches out a tentative hand and places it on Albert's forehead. Albert rumbles. Joe jumps back.

"He's just purring," I say. "He's not going to hurt you."

"How do you know?"

I glance at my dragon. "I just do."

"Great. I feel so much better." But he's smiling. And his hand is back on Albert, gently petting him. "Now, it is super critical we figure out what this Albert-dragon can *do*."

Do? "Huh?"

"Dragons can have a wide variety of skills."

"How do you know that?"

"Haven't you ever played Dungeons and Dragons?" Joe asks. "No? Well, me neither because my brothers won't let me in the game, but I have *overheard* a lot. Different dragons have different skills. The question is, what special dragon skills does *Albert* have?"

I glance at Albert, who appears to be listening intently to Joe. "He can make himself into a cat. Other than that, I have no idea what skills he might or might not have," I admit. "I don't even really know what you're talking about."

Joe throws up his hands, exasperated. "Can he fly? Can he exhale sleeping gas? Can he spew acid? Some dragons can breathe poison or turn a victim to ice or exercise mind control. *Skills* that can help us. Like I said." His expression is dead serious.

"Wait a minute. *Mind* control?"

"Of course. Albert, can you do any of those things?"

Albert glares at him and snorts a few puffs of smoke. "I don't think he wants to go to dragon school," I comment.

Joe is about to launch into a defense of why we need to know these things about our dragon, I *know* he is, when a stray cat emerges from beneath the holly shrubs. He's gray and white, tattered ears flat, fangs bared, and hissing like a popped balloon. He is not pleased to find us invading his territory.

"It's okay, kitty," I say. I'm about to shoo him away when I notice Albert's terrified expression. *Wait a minute. You're a dragon and this is an eight-pound scrawny, neglected cat!* Albert whimpers. How embarrassing.

Joe giggles. "He's freaking out."

"You're fine, Albert," I say soothingly. "This cat is not going to hurt you." The cat inches forward in a full Halloween pose. Albert scooches behind me, shaking ears to tail, useless little puffs of steam rising from his nose. What happened to the dragon who defended me at Mia's house? Or against Slack?

"Time to take off, cat," I say gently, nudging the stray. The cat takes one meaningless swipe at my tennis shoe and, content in his victory, saunters off into the underbrush.

Joe buries his head in his hands. "Our dragon is a lemon," he moans. "No skills at *all*. What a world!"

Albert shrugs this off, shaking his wings out, all nonchalant like nothing happened. He curls into a tight ball and closes his eyes. Joe and I return to the bench, and Joe pulls some oranges from the bottomless backpack. When I glance at Albert, he's a speck of a snoring kitten. I gently lift him from the wet ground and snuggle him in my lap.

"If my brothers knew I had a dragon," Joe says, holding an orange out to me, "their heads would explode, and after that they'd be so jealous."

"Do they really not let you play D&D with them?" I ask.

"Didn't you know?" Joe asks sarcastically. "I'm invisible. My brothers don't even say hi to me in the hallways!"

"Well, even if that is true," I say quickly, "*I* see you. And I'm really glad you are here."

Joe shoves a segment of orange into his mouth and casts his eyes down. I think he might be blushing. "On the positive side," he says, "being invisible makes disappearing super easy."

I nod. "Yeah. Helicopter parents would be a nightmare."

"It would be the worst! Like Samantha, whose mom still walks her to homeroom every day."

"And carries her backpack!" I add. "That would be mortifying."

We take a moment to feel sorry for Samantha, who might be lower down on the middle school food chain than we are, which is saying something. In our comfortable silence, I blurt, "I like black holes because they might be a way to rearrange time and make things different. And

I want to make things different." My dad dying. My mom falling apart. Mia ditching me.

"You do?" Joe asks, orange juice shiny on his chin.

And something in his face gives me pause. I glance at my new friend and down at Albert and think I might not want *everything* to be different. What if right now, in this exact moment, things are pretty good in a totally bizarre kind of way? "Maybe not everything," I reply.

Joe grins, and I smile back. As we sit there in the drizzle, dark angry clouds swirling above, I cover Albert with my hands, a protective shield. He might be a lemon, but he's *my* lemon.

"I think we can still get into the library without a dragon," I say finally.

"How?"

"Using our wits."

"That's a great plan, Cassie."

"Don't be sarcastic, Joe."

"Give me the details," he demands.

"I don't have any," I reply.

"So we just march on up and ask if we can see the dragon box from 1850 or whatever?"

"Well, *you* march up, not me. My face is plastered all over Lewiston."

Joe thinks about it and shrugs. "Why not? Weirder things have happened."

That's the spirit! My plan may not be much of a plan, but at least it is better than sitting here in the increasingly heavy rain. "Come on," I say, nudging Joe. "Let's do this."

Chapter 29

DUNGEONS AND DRAGONS AND ARCHIVES

THE UNIVERSITY LIBRARY, nicknamed the Starlight, is stunning enough to make folks who can't spell "book" swoon. The building is only two years old, a steel-and-glass structure that somehow matches the importance of the pursuit of knowledge within. Even against the perpetual Lewiston grayness, the Starlight glimmers like the Emerald City.

Inside, the building smells of the lavender that fills the surrounding gardens. There's a soothing fountain in the lobby featuring silver stars and moons. Voices are hushed in reverence, and students are careful not to step too loudly across the marble floors.

Joe pauses at the entrance. "I love it here," he whispers. "It makes me dizzy but in a good way."

I nod in agreement, pulling my hood tighter around my face. This is all over in a heartbeat if someone figures out who I am. The entry to the library is barred by a turnstile that requires a proper student identification card in order to enter. To the left is a desk manned by a young student eating an apple and reading a hardbound book, the cover of which I cannot see. When he laughs, bits of peel fly out of his mouth. He doesn't appear to care.

Joe takes a deep breath, psyching himself up to ask this apple-eating student library-guard if we may pass.

"You can do this," I whisper. "No problem."

"Easy for you to say," Joe replies without looking at me. Cracking his knuckles, he exhales sharply and strides toward the desk. I edge close enough to listen.

"Hi," Joe says brightly.

The apple eater glances up. "Hi yourself," he says. "Can I help you? You look a little short to be a college student."

Joe laughs too loudly at this joke, which, from the look on Apple Eater's face, is not actually a joke and more of an observation. "Can't help how tall we are, can we?" Joe answers. "Genes and all that. Hey, is that the Dungeons and Dragons Candlekeep Mysteries guide you're reading?" He points to the book. Apple Eater picks it up, revealing the cover. More dragons. Great.

"Sure is," he says with a grin. "Why? Do you play?"

I hold my breath, waiting to see if Joe will launch into the stories of his older brothers and how they never let him play but because he eavesdrops so much it's like he does know how to play. But instead he just gives a vague nod and asks Apple Eater his opinion on the seventeen mystery-themed role-playing adventures laid out in the book. I, of course, have no idea what they are talking about, but this does not stop me from being super impressed with Joe's ability to work this situation to his advantage.

Before long he turns to me with a big smile and waves me forward. "Stan looked up the box and it's here. He's going to let us see it. How excellent is that?"

Very excellent. I like this apple-eating Stan person quite a bit right now. Albert wiggles in my pocket but settles back down. I repeat a calming mantra in my head in the hopes that it reaches him and he won't make a scene. We simply cannot afford a scene.

Stan abandons his post, leaving his D&D book and apple core on the desk. We trail after him to the far end of the library and down two stories in an elevator. My heart pounds as I try to angle away from Stan in the tiny enclosed space so he can't get a good look at my face. But Joe keeps up the D&D banter, which he is obviously enjoying, and Stan casts barely a glance in my direction. We land with a thud and exit into a wide high-ceilinged warehouse that seems entirely unrelated to the Starlight vibe two floors above. Floor-to-ceiling metal shelves are stacked high with labeled boxes. The temperature is cool and the air dry.

"We're looking for row eighteen, shelving unit six, box seven hundred and forty-two," Stan says, striding down the aisle between the shelving. As we go, motion-sensitive lighting sparks to life above us, casting a harsh green glow over our progress. We run to keep up.

Stan stops abruptly. "Here we go." Using a ladder on wheels, he pulls down a box from an upper shelf and places it on a table in the aisle. "When you're done, just leave it here. It's part of the night crew's job to put stuff away." He snickers at this, as if pulling night crew duty is some sort of punishment. "All right, good? I gotta get back upstairs before someone notices I'm gone."

He gives Joe an enthusiastic fist bump. He doesn't instruct us on how to handle the archival materials in the box. He doesn't ask that we check with him before we go. He just leaves us there. It's pretty great. We wait until the elevator doors close before regarding each other with amazement.

"I didn't think it would be that easy," I say with wonder.

"Easy?" Joe counters. "I had to go deep into my memory banks for some of that D&D stuff. Like, *deep*."

"You were perfect," I say.

A blush rises on Joe's cheeks, and he mutters something that I think is a thanks. It happens that I know a thing or two about going for a long time without registering on the world's radar. I know it doesn't feel good. Pointing out where Joe is good at things is not so hard. I resolve to do it more.

But for now we tear into the box, flinging the cardboard top aside and plunging our hands into the contents. The barcoded archival folders inside are labeled *Lewiston Local History*. There is a note indicating many of the documents were water-damaged in the Lewiston Public Library flood, and in some cases materials were a total loss. There is a list of the box's contents, including the sketches.

We dig in. The first folder we open contains newspaper clippings covering the 1890 founding of the university. There's also a printed booklet from the first graduation held in 1892. We pull out more folders.

"Do you see them?" I ask, peering into the box.

"No," Joe responds, "but look at *this*." He passes me a handwritten index card listing who has accessed the box in the last two years. There are only two names on the card.

Sheldon Slack. And *Ellen Asher*. But her name only appears once, the day after Joe and I got caught in the storm and found Albert in the dumpster. She must have hoped the diary had magically resurfaced. She is nothing if not thorough.

I pull a stack of folders from the box, and we begin to comb through them, looking for the sketches. But the folder labeled *Forest Scenes* is empty.

"These materials are not supposed to leave the archives," Joe shouts, offended on behalf of the missing pages. But it seems this archive has a bad habit of losing things.

Something occurs to me that is a little radical. "What if Miss Asher *stole* them?" I ask. "Maybe she figured they were important. And she was the last one here."

"Miss Asher stealing archives?" Joe whispers, aghast at the very idea.

"I don't know if she did," I explain, "but *if* she did, I bet I know where she'd hide them."

Joe narrows his gaze. "We have to break into that drawer *again*?"

"It's a bummer," I mutter, shoulders sagging. *And* a problem. The library is closed and we can't exactly skip up to Miss Asher's house and ask to borrow her key so we can take what she already took.

"Well," Joe replies, resigned, "no one ever said solving a mystery involving dragons and dimension-changing wormhole rip-thingies was going to be easy."

It occurs to me that Joe and I keep switching who is in charge of keeping up morale. When he's deflated, I egg him on, and when I am, he does the same for me. We make a good team. And in this case, he's right. I can't give up trying to figure out what is going on just because it's hard.

We leave the archival box on the table as instructed and board the elevator. On the main floor, Albert begins to wiggle, and I scratch between his ears in the hopes of calming him enough that we can get out of the Starlight without incident. It is only when I pass a glass panel and catch a glimpse of my reflection that I realize the problem isn't Albert. My hood is down and the blue raincoat is knotted around my waist. Everyone can see my face.

And they do. I feel the eyes scanning me, trying to figure out why I look familiar, trying to place that unexpected flash of recognition. Quickly, I pull up my hood and yank the strings to hide as much of myself as I can. But it is too late. Heads cock curiously, thumbs fly. How long until the Lewiston police receive a report about a possible sighting? Not long enough. I grab Joe and bolt for the door.

"Cassie! What the heck?" Joe yells, tripping over his own feet to keep up.

But the look on my face tells him everything he needs to know. He picks up the pace and we fly out the exit, right past Stan, who, face buried in his book, does not even glance up.

This won't stop, not until they find me and Albert. And telling them Albert is nothing to fear will not matter. We are being hunted.

We. Albert and me.

And that is the moment when I realize something. We have to get Albert home, no matter what.

And I plan to go with him.

Chapter 30

BREAKING AND ENTERING

I DO NOT SHARE MY DECISION with Joe. He will only try to talk me out of it. Besides, we have things to do. By the time we reach the library, it is late in the day and the parking lot is deserted. Which is good. There won't be anyone around to catch us breaking in.

Normally I would never commit a crime against a library, but these are desperate times. I wish we had a paper clip, not that I know how to use one to pick a lock. But the lock on the library entrance is electronic anyway and would laugh in the face of a paper clip. We sneak around to the side of the building and hunker down in the shadows. We don't have a lot of time. Those people in the Starlight have probably already contacted the Lewiston police with sighting information. It's even possible that we were followed here. I push these thoughts aside. They are messing with my concentration.

"Now what?" asks Joe.

"Let me think," I respond.

He pauses and shuffles his feet. "Are you done thinking yet?"

"You don't happen to know the code to open the door, do you?"

"Nope."

"And you don't have a key."

"Sure I do. For my bike lock and my house."

"Not helpful."

"I didn't think so. Cassie, the more I think about it, the more I'm sure we need those sketches. Along with the map, it gives us a real shot at finding the rip."

There is a small window at ground level that leads to the library basement. I glance at it. Joe frowns. "Miss Asher will kill us," he says, gesturing at the window. "I am one hundred percent sure of that."

He's right. She won't be pleased. But I don't see any other way we can get into the building.

"Do you think the building has an alarm?" I ask.

Joe scoffs. "Are you kidding me? Remember the fire door? They won't even pay for heat that works!" He has a point. I edge toward the window, picking up a small rock. At first I just tap gently on the window. Nothing happens. It's glass! It's supposed to break! I mean, I broke Joe's window with a pebble!

"Give me that," Joe says, grabbing the rock from my hand. In one swift move, he smashes it against the glass and the pane shatters inward. It's loud. *Really* loud. "Oops." We freeze, waiting to see if police or weird FBI agents swarm the building. Nothing happens, but we wait an extra minute just to be sure. Okay. Here we go. Using a stick, I sweep aside all the remaining glass so we can safely squeeze through the window. It's about seven feet to the floor, which doesn't sound high, but it is when you have to jump it. I land with a thud. Albert pops his head out to see what is happening. Just beginning a life of crime, little guy. No big deal. Gulp.

"Oof!" Joe lands beside me, glancing around the dim basement.

We're *in*.

The basement is full of dusty boxes, discarded furniture, old computer components, and shelves of books from ancient times, like five years ago or something. Looming in the shadows is a television on a wheelie cart with a VCR beneath it. Doesn't Miss Asher ever throw *anything* away? And I only know what a VCR is because Dad had one when I was little. I ruined it by stuffing my peanut butter and jelly sandwich in the slot meant for the tape. But in my defense, it is *perfectly* sandwich shaped, and I just had to see what would happen. What happened was I ruined the VCR, and Dad said it was okay, but I could see from his eyes he didn't mean it.

We gingerly pick our way around the old and forgotten stuff to the stairs. The quiet is not the good kind like in the botanical garden but the creepy kind that makes the little hairs on my arms stand at attention. I push open the door at the top of the stairs inch by inch, peering out to ensure nobody is there waiting to grab me or Albert or Joe, although Joe is the only one without some sort of bounty on his head. Honestly, I don't know why he doesn't abandon us right now and go back to his house and his family and all those cookies. But then I remember his lousy brothers don't even let him play Dungeons & Dragons, and, believe me, Joe would be excellent at that game. I guess I understand why he's still here, risking his freedom. It gives me the confidence to plow forward.

"Anyone out there?" Joe whispers, looking over my shoulder.

"Coast is clear," I reply. The door gives and we step tentatively into the empty, semi-dark library. I glance toward the reference desk, half expecting to see Miss Asher looming there in the shadows. But the place is still and silent, as if time has stopped. Joe rushes ahead of me.

"Come on," he urges. Albert, equally excited to get going, leaps free and scampers after Joe. He throws a look back at me full of judgment. How can I be so slow? *Okay. I'm coming.*

Joe plows past the comfortable reading lounges and a cluster of desks, kicking a chair out of the way and practically launching himself at Miss Asher's desk. Albert is hot on his heels, as if he somehow knows what is going on. Or maybe he just can't resist Joe's untied shoelace.

Like a batter sliding into first, Joe throws himself into her chair and tugs the drawer. Locked. *Of course.* His shoulders sag. I appreciate that he expected the universe to have left the drawer open for us, but he is kidding himself. The universe is uninterested. This is confirmed when I dump out the paper clips only to discover the key is gone. The leading edge of despair lodges in my belly.

"Just use a paper clip," Joe suggests.

Easy for him to say. He's a spectator. Albert, completely consumed with Joe's shoelace, leaps and rolls along, and also does not do a good job helping. "Fine," I mutter. Choosing one of the large clips, I unbend it until it is mostly straight. I have no idea what I'm doing, but whenever I see people pick locks on TV, they just stick the paper clip in and wiggle it around, all while appearing to be deep in concentration. So that's what I do.

It doesn't work. Joe rolls his eyes. "Try harder," he suggests.

"Why don't you do it?" I snap.

"Because you're better at this sort of thing."

"How do you know that?" I ask. "The drawer is still locked."

"Because my palms are sweating and yours aren't, which means you are less nervous, which means you can focus."

I want to argue, but I don't even know where to start. And sometimes it's not worth it. I yank on the drawer hard in total frustration, and much to my surprise, it gently glides open.

"I told you," Joe says with a grin. Albert leaps straight up from the floor and noses his way into the drawer. I can almost hear what he is thinking. *Treats?*

"No treats," I say sternly. "In a few minutes, okay? When we get out of here?" His little face collapses with disappointment, but we are kind of in a rush. At some point we are going to get caught.

"Take him," I say, plucking Albert out of the drawer and handing him to Joe, who tucks the squirmy kitten up under his chin. The drawer is empty, but the pages could be wedged in the back. The only way to check is to bend my elbow at an unnatural angle and jam my arm inside. My fingers brush up against something, but I can't quite grasp it.

Joe makes goofy faces at Albert, who bats at his nose, having gone from bored to delighted in a millisecond. I might be stuck. It will be bad to be caught in the library when we are not supposed to be here. It will be much worse to be caught wedged into Miss Asher's locked drawer. Finally I pinch the corner of a page with my fingers. When I yank my arm out, some skin comes off.

"Ow! Great!"

"You got it?" Joe asks anxiously. He grabs the papers from my hands before I can even answer and takes off into the stacks. Albert cavorts after him, leaping at invisible flying mice or whatever. I find the two of them back on the floor in the medieval history section, Joe with his phone flashlight on, studying the pages. Albert weaves in and out of Joe's legs.

"Well?" I demand. "Does it help us find the rip?"

But before Joe can answer, there is noise outside the library.

Voices.

Chapter 31

UNWELCOME COMPANY

JOE GLANCES AT ME. "Uh-oh."

That's an understatement. We scramble to the edge of the stacks for a clear view of two women entering the library. It's the same two women who followed Slack after he argued with Mayor Diaz! So much has happened since then, I kind of forgot about them, but here they are, dark suits, sunglasses, shiny badges.

"The police captain said the tip specifically placed the girl here at the library?" asks the one with red hair and invisible eyebrows.

"Ah, Agent Dana," replies the one with the sharp gray bob, shaking her head. "Just because they said it does not make it fact. These local departments in out-of-the-way places are usually not that helpful."

Agent Dana snorts. "Agent Fox," she says, pretending to be shocked. "How can you say such things?"

Agent Fox from Miss Asher's notebook? The one who stopped her in the street looking for the diary of Edward Tenbrook all those years ago? She's older now and with a new partner, but it has to be the same person.

Agent Fox offers a sly smile to Agent Dana. "Listen, I've seen some unbelievable stuff since I raised my hand to work these cases. And the reason these local departments end up not being so helpful is that they don't want to believe that dragons . . . *dragons* . . . are real." Agent Fox pulls out her flashlight and flicks it on. The beam penetrates the gloom, illuminating the dust hanging in the air. "And if we tell them they are, in fact, real . . . well . . . that just causes all sorts of problems and makes our job more complicated."

Agent Dana watches her. "And that's the reason we keep everyone in the dark?"

"Exactly, Agent Dana. People are happier if we protect their version of reality, even if they don't know it."

"Slack knows it," Dana says, "and he's not happy."

"There is always one," Fox replies with a sigh. "Someone

who does not get the message that he is better off keeping his mouth shut. The government will go a long way to protect its secrets."

"I understand," Dana says.

"I know you do," answers Fox. "That's why you are here."

In response, Agent Dana grins, big and wide and satisfied, and I can tell she *likes* this job. A lot. I mean, dragons. But what *else*? I find myself enormously curious, but this is not the time for a question-and-answer. The two women fan out, flashlights on, searching.

"Have you ever seen one?" Agent Dana asks quietly. "A dragon?"

Agent Fox shakes her head. "No. But it's high on the list of things I *do* want to see. It might even be on the top."

"Me too," Dana replies, a little breathless.

"There are sightings once in a while," Fox says. "People who are sure they saw one, and we always go and check it out, but so far, nothing."

I feel Joe tense beside me, and this reels me back in. One false move, one sneeze or wiggly cat, and we are done for. The only way out of the library is the way we came in, and right now Dana and Fox block our route.

There has to be another way.

I nudge Joe and gesture toward the back of the library.

Joe shakes his head ever so slightly. No. Way. If I could, I'd explain that if we can get to the stairs that lead to the library's second floor, we can get to the roof. But talking is right out. Instead I grab him by the hood and drag him behind me. It's kind of a miracle that Fox and Dana don't see or hear us, but they have already decided we're not actually here, and that works in our favor for the moment. It won't last. They aren't idiots.

From the roof, we can jump to the neighboring building and escape like superheroes. It can work. I mean, there are photographs of black holes, and there are dragons and other extraordinary things. *Anything* can happen, even us taking a death-defying leap through the air.

But I don't mention any of this to Joe. Not yet, anyway.

We barrel up the narrow stairs to the roof exit. Joe, huffing behind me, says he never imagined today would end up like this.

"What did you think was going to happen?" I ask, breathless.

"Not this," he insists. "You better go faster."

"I don't think I can," I wheeze. My lungs might burst right out of my chest. Nothing in PE prepared me for all this running. At the top, I hit the metal door with my shoulder and it flies open.

The roof is nothing interesting, an expanse of chipped concrete and old heating and air-conditioning equipment, ominous in the lengthening shadows. A chest-high fence runs all around the roof to keep innocents from tumbling off. I run to the far side and stare down. While jumping the space between this building and the next would be no big deal for Supergirl, it's a little intimidating for a regular person like me. My mouth is suddenly pasty and dry. Joe peers over the edge.

"We'll die," he says flatly. "That's just physics."

That is not the answer I want. It won't be long before Fox and Dana figure out we are up here and things get complicated. Albert will try to protect us and end up in the hands of secret government agents. Or worse. How would we even begin to explain everything that has happened? Even if I tried, they wouldn't listen. I'm just a kid. No one really listens to kids.

"Has anyone ever, you know, defied physics?" I ask hopefully.

"You mean, like, escaped the pull of gravity? Sure. In *outer* space."

"So not helpful," I reply.

"I think it's over," Joe says glumly. "I don't see a way out of this. We need to turn ourselves in."

That Joe has a point makes me instantly nauseous. But Miss Asher chooses this moment to appear in the doorway to the roof, clutching the yellow notebook to her chest. Was she alerted to a break-in? How mad is she? How did she get around the agents and get up here in the first place? Or did they send her?

"Kids," she says, her eyes bright. "Are you safe? Are you okay?"

I nod, afraid to open my mouth.

Miss Asher exhales sharply. "Good. Listen to me. I know you read the journal, but there are things not written in there, parts of the story you don't understand." That's actually inaccurate. We don't understand *anything*. "After Sheldon and I found Edward's diary, we chased down every random lead, every possibility, every dragon-related rumor and urban myth."

She laughs sadly, moving a step toward us. "I thought it was all a bit of fun, something to distract my friend from his sorrow. His twin brother was dying, but his grief was bigger than I understood, because while I knew Edward's story was a fantasy, Sheldon *believed* it."

I flash on that moment in Joe's kitchen, how he never questioned the outrageous tale I told, like Miss Asher questioned Sheldon. Her gaze seems haunted in the fading light.

"When the storms came," she continues, "*just* as Edward had described them, together with what you told me about Albert, I had to reevaluate. It seems inter-dimensional dragon travel wreaks havoc on the weather after all." I think she is making a joke, but no one laughs.

"But Sheldon never found a rip, right?" Joe asks urgently.

"No," Miss Asher says. "He tried, but it's hard to find something when you don't know where to look."

But *we* know. Sort of. Miss Asher gazes up at the gloomy sky. Her eyes are damp. "Sheldon wanted to find the dragons so badly," she says, "to force the universe to give him back what it took. But bad things happen in life. There is not always a reason. Sometimes it's just random."

In my pocket, Albert tenses. I rest a hand on him, but he doesn't settle. Miss Asher continues, edging closer to us. "Sheldon has never stopped hunting. I begged him to give up his quest, but he refused. He would hunt these dragons to the ends of the earth and beyond if necessary. It was no longer about Cyrus. And he doesn't care if the dragons die, just as Edward described. He's blinded by obsession, by some twisted need to fulfill a mission he set for himself years ago."

Maybe it's because he doesn't like all this dragon-hunting talk, or maybe he's just bored, but for whatever reason, Albert springs out of my pocket. Just looking at him brings a surge of love bubbling up in my chest. His whiskers twitch and his tail swishes. When I stoop to pick him up, he scampers away, sitting midway between us and Miss Asher, tail wrapped around his feet, and I swear he smiles. The smoke fills the air before I have time to warn Miss Asher. Joe grabs on to me, but at least he doesn't yelp. But Miss Asher sure does.

"This. Cannot. Be. Happening."

Albert emerges, rumbling and snorting, pawing gently at the ground, plumes of steam escaping his snout. Miss Asher presses the notebook to her heart. "It really is a *dragon*," she whispers. "Edward's story is *true*."

Beyond Miss Asher, the door flies open, and Agents Dana and Fox appear. And even though they believe in dragons, they are still totally unprepared for seeing one in real life.

"Oh my . . . It's a . . ." Dana scrambles for her phone, but in a panic fumbles it. I wonder who she intends to call. She drops to her hands and knees, yelling at us to not move, searching for the fallen phone, while Fox stands like a statue, jaw hanging open, because she is suddenly within ten feet of a real live dragon. I honestly did not expect them to freak out so completely. It seems out of character.

"Agents!" Miss Asher shouts. "I can explain."

But no one can really explain, except maybe the universe, and she's not talking. We have a single moment to escape, and once it is gone, I cannot say what will happen, but I know it will not be good.

Albert, get us out of here.

Okay, Cassie.

In a single stride, Albert is beside Joe, nudging him toward me. "What's he doing?" Joe asks, voice shaky.

No idea. But I asked him to get us out of here. Joe and I are now shoulder-to-shoulder, Albert behind us. Do I suspect what is coming when Albert grasps us each firmly by the collar with clawed feet? Possibly, but he definitely takes Joe by surprise.

"He is *not*," Joe yells. But he is! Holding us tight, Albert sprints toward the edge of the roof. "We are going to die! Our dragon is a lemon! He can't fly!"

Joe squeezes his eyes shut, but I force mine to stay open. We crash over the edge, our shins smacking the railing, and plummet toward the sidewalk. Miss Asher screams something I can't understand. Fox and Dana scream too. Time slows down, moving like cold syrup from the bottle. Joe howls, his legs bicycling, flailing for purchase when there is none to be had. I feel Albert's hot puffs of breath on my neck, the intense rush of his beating wings. The sidewalk zooms toward us. Albert swerves and wobbles, clutching us tighter. He lurches left. And then, as if an invisible trampoline has lofted us into the early-evening sky, we are *airborne*.

I let out an involuntary shout as we soar up and over the rooftops. "Joe! Open your eyes! We're flying!"

When he does, he whoops with delight. "We're really flying!"

Under our shoes is Community Park, the low buildings and playing fields of Lewiston Senior High School, the main firehouse and police station, the pond where we used to feed the ducks. The lights in the university dormitories blink on as the day fades. Albert picks up speed and wind whistles in our ears.

"He DOES have skills!" Joe shouts. "He can fly!"

Tilting right, Albert curves toward the coast, the smell of ocean air rising to meet us. Albert swoops down close to the water, cruising right above the waves. The spray is cold on our faces as we race skyward again. As Albert barrel-rolls, we hang on for dear life, the sky and the water rotating around us at a dizzying speed.

"Tell him to land at the lighthouse at Pirates Point," Joe yells.

Pirates Point is a rocky spit that sticks out like a finger into the rough and cold Pacific Ocean. Many a trader has met his end at Pirates Point. A postcard-perfect white lighthouse sits on the very tip of the spit, a relic from the days when people used to ply these waters despite the risk. But when Joe said we should land at the lighthouse, I don't think he meant *on* the lighthouse. Which is where we now perch, clinging to Albert so we don't tumble to the ground below.

Albert preens in the stiff breeze blowing off the ocean. I guess if you make bad weather, you eventually grow to like it. At least it's not raining. Joe hands me his phone, flashlight on. "Hold that!" he yells. As I do, he fumbles around for Edward's sketches crammed in his pockets. One of them is immediately snatched up by the wind and blown away.

"Not good," Joe growls. "Bring the phone closer." The pool of light illuminates delicate drawings of a cluster of trees, with nothing to indicate where these particular trees might *be*. But I recognize them. It feels like a gift from my father.

"Mercy Grove!" I shout.

Mercy Grove is deep in the Arcata wilderness, a cluster of ancient redwood trees that form a perfect circle as if purposefully planted. My father loved it there and we visited often. Dad said it was a magical place. He said it had an energy he couldn't fully understand. I never heard him say that about any other patch of forest, so it stuck with me.

The hike to the grove is up a narrow creek bed snaking through a fifty-foot-deep vertical-walled canyon. The canyon walls are completely covered in a dazzling display of primal ferns, showing off with every shade of green the eye can absorb. The sounds of civilization are replaced with birds and insects, and the breeze in the trees. The water in the creek is icy cold as the sun will sometimes poke through the fog, creating a fan of perforated light. Had fairies or pixies appeared in the air on any of our visits, I would not have been at all surprised. *Magical.*

"Are you sure?" Joe shouts.

I nod. I can see Dad's face in my memory and hear his words. Mercy Grove is where we need to go. We hold on tight to Albert and once again lift off into the sky. Keeping the coastline on our left, we surge northward. Mercy Grove is about ten miles from the lighthouse and inland. If we turn in at the mouth of the Lewiston Creek, it should lead us directly there.

"Albert!" I yell. "That way!"

I point northeast, and Albert banks hard, and of course

Joe and I scream, but it's the good kind of scream, like we are on a roller coaster.

There are miles of nothing north of Lewiston, just the ocean giving way to thickly forested hills. As we swoop and roll like birds riding the air current, I notice small lakes surrounded by cliffs of pale limestone, hidden from humanity. Nature goes on, whether we see it or not. Joe taps me on the shoulder.

"This is the most amazing thing that has ever happened to me," he shouts. "Thank you, Cassie."

"And you thought he was a lemon," I chide.

Joe grins, and despite everything, I grin back. And it occurs to me that I will miss Joe terribly when I go with Albert back to the dimension of the dragons.

Chapter 32

MERCY GROVE

AS THE SUN DROPS LOWER, I catch sight of the Lewiston Creek leading through the fern canyon and onto Mercy Grove, a ribbon of glassy water cutting through the forest. "Follow that stream," I instruct Albert, who banks wildly at my new directions. I think he's doing it on purpose. I think he thinks it's funny when we scream.

Down below, I sense animal eyes peering up at us and wondering what sort of weirdo bird we are. Definitely too big to be an eagle or a hawk. And way too many heads! How hideous! We drop, moving off from the creek and cruising right above the magnificent ancient trees.

Albert sets us down gently right in the middle of the circle of towering giants. The fading light filters through the canopy above, casting long shadows. The massive trees seem to lock arms, guardians against oncoming intruders. The energy within the circle is different, just as my dad recognized. It's charged somehow, *expectant*. The world around us hums with nocturnal animal life, squeaking and whistling and small feet crunching leaves.

Joe steps closer to me. "I'm not a big outdoorsy person," he says. "I mean, four people were killed by bears last year in North America. I know that puts the likely percentage of me being attacked by a bear at, like, basically zero. But still, I have to ask. Do you think there is anything here that, you know, might eat us?"

"You're with a *dragon*," I remind him. "What could possibly happen to you?"

"Remember, this dragon is afraid of stray cats," Joe replies.

"You will not be eaten," I clarify. There is nothing to fear here, at least not from the natural world. But eventually Dana and Fox will find us. After all, we flew here on a dragon. There is bound to be chatter. We have to find the rip, and soon.

Joe, as if reading my thoughts, asks me if I happen to

have a manual handy on how to promote interdimensional travel by finding and opening a rip to the dragon world. I snort. "I wish."

We study the Edward drawings for additional clues, but there is nothing helpful there. Great. We get all the way to the right spot but can't find the on/off switch. On the other hand, I have not allowed myself to think about what going through a rip will feel like. Will it be like falling into an active volcano? Or being tossed into space without a suit? Will it hurt? Will I, you know, disintegrate?

None of that matters, Cassie, if you can't find the rip!

Right. First things first. Find the rip and then worry about disintegrating. I turn in a slow circle, taking note of the trees. There are lots and lots of trees. My palms start to sweat. "We don't even know what we were looking for," I say. My voice is too loud in the silence.

"I know," Joe replies. "It's not like we've ever seen a rip before or anything."

But Albert *has*. That's how he got here in the first place. He *must* remember something. "I have an idea," I say.

"Good. Because I'm fresh out."

And that's when I notice Albert is hunched down, sagging against a massive tree trunk. His skin is dull and his breathing labored. I panic, rushing to him, and drop to my knees. His glazed eyes meet mine. Why doesn't he turn back into a cat?

"Albert!" I cry. "Change back!"

Can't, Cassie.

All I can think is he put out so much energy getting us here and now has none left to manage the shift back to his cat form. And as a dragon, he just grows weaker. We have to find that rip, and we have to do it now.

Joe is beside me, resting an open palm on Albert. "His heart is racing."

I take Albert's head in my hands, startled by how cool he is. It's not right. "We need to get you home. But we don't know how to find the rip, you know, the door to your world."

I can't say aloud that I intend to go with him. If Joe catches wind of my plan, it won't go over well. I try to push away the idea of Joe being alone after I'm gone and think only about the message I want Albert to receive.

Tell me how to find the rip. We will go through together. We will go home, where you will be okay.

With great effort, Albert pushes his leathery head into my chest, and as I scratch his ears, he wheezes. Does he hear me? Does he know I'm coming with him? Desperation sends my pulse sky high. It's a long moment before Albert pulls back. He closes his eyes, his long dark lashes resting on his cheeks. His shoulders rise and fall as he takes deep breaths of the forest air. Nothing happens

"What's he doing?" Joe whispers.

"I don't know," I reply.

Albert shudders, a flare of fire bursting from his snout. I leap to the side to avoid getting scorched. And suddenly a glittery mist rises from the golden blaze on his chest.

"Whoa," sputters Joe. He's right about that. We don't dare move as the mist begins to bend and morph, throwing off sparks and angling out and away from Albert. It stretches into a lopsided oval. The very trees themselves, the sturdy ancient giants, appear to bow down to the oval.

"I think it's the rip," Joe says quietly. "I think we could have looked for it forever and not found anything, because only Albert can open it with his super glitter."

The edges of the oval glow bright red. Through the oval I can see another forest. It's brighter and the tree bark is iridescent like soap bubbles. The colors are so vivid, they hurt my eyes. It's the forest from my dream. But in our forest the weather abruptly changes. Heavy rain starts to fall, undeterred by the protective canopy above. It's icy cold. Lightning cracks and shatters the quiet night. The oval glows and sparks. The trees bend lower.

"Definitely the rip!" Joe yells.

As the rain pelts down and the rip hovers, Albert opens his eyes. His gaze settles on me, beckoning, as he tries to stand. It is time to go.

And why wouldn't I? Dad is gone. Mom doesn't care about me. My best friend hates me. My classmates laugh at me. The best thing in my life is Albert. My head spins. There really is no good reason for me to stay.

"We need to help him!" I yell. Positioning ourselves so Albert can lean on us, we move him closer to the rip. It's not as bright as before, and the edges are ragged.

"It's losing integrity!" Joe shouts. "Hurry!"

But just as we are about to push Albert through the rip, with me right behind him, we are interrupted by a commotion on the trail.

Emerging from the darkness is Sheldon Slack, rainsoaked and disheveled, his orange coat streaked with mud from a fall he must have taken running down the steep, slick trail. His eyes quiver in his head, taking in the scene before him. Gasping for air, Slack can barely get his words out.

"Not so fast!" he screeches. "I've been searching for you *forever*! And you are not going anywhere!"

And somehow I just know he's not talking about me or Joe.

Chapter 33

DRAGON HUNTER

SHELDON SLACK, soggy and wild eyed, looks more like a vampire than ever. And the way he rubs his hands together, with clear delight and relish, he might actually be preparing to eat us.

"The pain and anguish you can alleviate with just your blood," says Slack, gaze locked tight on Albert. "Such a small sacrifice for the greater good. No one will ever have to go through what I did again."

As Slack steps closer to us, I notice something clutched in his hand, a silvery rectangular object. "A stun gun," Joe whispers. "A *taser*." This is getting completely out of hand. He intends to shock my weakened dragon into submission and kidnap him, just like Edward's awful family did to Alvina. But sacrificing himself to save us humans from pain and anguish is not Albert's responsibility. Nor any dragon's.

Without thinking, I scream, "Go, Albert! Go now!" and push him hard. The rip snaps and pops. But Albert, sensing the danger, digs in.

The vampire moves fast. In a flash, he has me in his grip, his arm locked around my neck, the taser inches from *my* skin. "You'll go nowhere unless you want to see harm come to your friend."

"Why are you doing this?" I whisper, clawing at his arm. "Albert can't bring back Cyrus."

Slack balks at his twin's name. "What do you know of Cyrus?" he asks, his hot breath on my neck.

"I know you lost him," I say. "And I know it hurts really badly."

"You know *nothing*," he hisses. "You are just a kid."

"My father died last year," I reply. "I *know*. But hurting Albert won't fix anything."

"Nice try, kid. But this dragon needs to be studied. He needs to be *used*."

"But Albert can't stay here. It's killing him."

"I don't *care*." Out of the corner of my eye, I see Joe,

immobilized with fear, Albert leaning on him hard. I struggle, but it's pointless. The vampire holds me fast.

"Please, Albert," I gasp. "Please go. Joe, make him go."

But Albert's eyes burn, and I know he is not leaving me, certainly not to save himself. He hisses, low and angry, flames flickering from between his jagged teeth. The vampire quakes in his waterlogged shoes. He's terrified. And he probably should be.

"Don't you try to intimidate me, dragon!" Slack shouts, his voice cracking. "One false move and this girl is history. You're mine now, no matter what, the hard way or the easy way."

Albert moves forward as if he summoning new energy out of nothing, as if floating above the ground. Slack, still holding me, backs up into the massive trunk of a redwood tree. He shakes uncontrollably. Albert advances, his hiss turning into a guttural growl, his eyes narrowing to slits.

"I'll do it!" Slack yells. "I will! Don't test me!" Albert is so close now. His muscles ripple with tension, the heat coming off him in waves. Slack tightens his grip on my neck. Stars float in my field of vision, weaving and dodging. My legs wobble.

Albert focuses on Slack, a disorienting aura of calm settling in around him. Slowly, with pinpoint precision, as if he has done this a million times before, Albert exhales a stream of gas directly into the vampire's pale face. And just like that, Slack collapses in a heap at my feet.

I stagger forward. Joe whoops and hollers. "Albert has *more* skills! Sleeping gas! That is awesome!"

His celebration is cut short by Albert crumpling to the ground. The edges of the rip are closing in. And there is noise on the trail, coming from the same direction as the sleeping Slack did.

This has to happen now. We hoist Albert up and shuffle toward the rip. The wind howls around us, a tight circle of me, Albert, and Joe, everything in the world that matters to me. I place both palms flat on the golden blaze in the middle of Albert's chest. He leans his forehead to mine, rumbling, huffing. His wings pulse weakly, but I keep my hands pressed to the golden blaze. Albert's eyes, the same mossy-green ones I first saw in that smoldering dumpster, close.

We go now, Cassie?

But it is Joe who speaks next. "I know you want to go with him, but please stay here," he says, clutching my arm. "I have this feeling when I wake up every day, it's like dread, because I know I have to go through another day, and it will be like the day before, and the day before was awful, and kids will mock me or pretend I don't exist, and both are really bad. But since our adventures started, that feeling is gone. I like who I am around you. You're my best friend. You *can't* leave."

His words stop me fast. I like who I am around Joe too. It's as if he has given me permission to be myself, to say out loud the words that usually are stuck in my head. It is nothing like being friends with Mia, which mostly doesn't feel good. This is different. A sharp pain in my heart takes my breath away. It's almost as if I am splitting in two. I think about the video of Joe talking to himself, how Mia and her friends laughed. Can I leave him to that, after all he has done for me and Albert? How can I choose between my best friend and my dragon? What sort of universe would make a girl do that? But I *do* have to choose.

Sensing my sudden reluctance, Albert nudges me, a plume of fire erupting from his flared nostrils. I wrap my arms around his neck, feeling his heat.

We go now, Cassie?

I can't, Albert. There are people here who need me.

Albert's shoulders heave, and a ragged breath escapes him. Our eyes hold each other fast.

With great effort, he places a clawed foot on my heart and taps ever so gently.

Cassie is good.

I wrap my arms around him as best I can. "I love you more than anything," I whisper. "And I will love you forever, every single day. We will be okay. You and me. I promise."

"Cassie, the *rip*," Joe says urgently. It is barely there now.

Reluctantly, I untangle myself. Albert presses his forehead into mine one last time. And then my sweet kitten, my brave dragon, turns and disappears through the rip. It sparks one last time and vanishes into thin air.

On cue, the rain ceases, the wind dies, and the clouds make way to reveal a bright full moon rising in a night sky. It is as if Albert was never here.

Joe catches me when my knees finally buckle.

Chapter 34

AND JUST LIKE THAT

A YOUNG COUPLE, shoes muddy, college sweatshirts soaked through, emerges from the shadows to find me propped up against a tree, Joe keeping me upright, and a man who looks suspiciously like a vampire crumpled in a heap at our feet. To their credit, they don't freak out.

"We were night hiking," the woman says, pushing a clump of dark wet hair back off her forehead. "There's nothing like the fern canyon on a night with a full moon."

"And we thought we saw . . . something in the sky," the guy adds, brows furrowed.

"We thought we saw a . . . well, never mind. Then that

storm kicked up. Crazy weather we are having. Are you two okay?"

The guy stares at Slack. "Is he dead?" he asks calmly, like this is just another normal walk in the woods in the dark of night during a storm, which maybe it is for these two.

Joe nudges Slack with his toe. "No," he says casually. "Just unconscious." We have no idea how long the sleeping gas lasts or what its long-term effects are, and we can't ask Albert because he's gone.

Albert. I sniffle. But I don't want to have to tell anything to these people even though they seem perfectly nice. The less known about Albert the better. Slack isn't the first person to come up with the idea of using dragons for his own ends, and he won't be the last. I steel myself to be tough.

Sensing their confusion about the whole scene, Joe launches into a story about how we were working on a project for school, something about forest ecology and various fern species, when we got hopelessly lost and ended up here. And no, we don't know the fainted guy.

"He just showed up and then kind of fell over and passed out," Joe says with a shrug. "Too much fresh air, maybe?"

The woman kneels beside Slack, wondering aloud if he might be diabetic or have some other medical condition.

She checks his wrist for a medical alert bracelet but, finding none, commences to dig through his pockets.

"Sheldon Slack," she says, pointing her flashlight at the man's driver's license. "He's thirty years old and lives in Lewiston."

Sheldon Slack stirs. "Did someone say my name?" he asks, his eyes unfocused and vague.

"Are you okay?" the woman asks, helping him to sit up. He glances at us, but there is no flash of recognition.

More crunchy footsteps on the trail. A park ranger emerges from the dark, her flashlight beam cutting through the night. "What's going on here?" she demands. "Is everyone all right? Night hiking is not a good idea. I don't know why I have to keep telling people that."

The couple explains that they always hike the fern canyon when there is a full moon because the rumor is that fairies who live there only come out during the full moon.

The park ranger sighs deeply. "Fairies? Really?"

"It might be true," Joe blurts. "There are things in the world that are . . . well . . . un*expected*."

"Do not tell me you two were up here searching for fairies too?" the ranger asks. "FYI, there are no fairies in the Arcata wilderness. Or anywhere, if we are being honest. And *who* is that?" She points to Slack, sitting in the mud.

"That's what we were telling you," says the guy. He explains that while they were hiking they thought they saw . . . something . . . and followed the trail up to the grove to check it out, only to find us, two lost kids, and this Sheldon Slack guy. Joe and I stay quiet, nodding along in agreement.

"What do *you* think you saw?" the ranger asks pointedly. "Because I thought I saw . . . well, never mind about that. It was probably an eagle. Is everyone okay?"

Slack staggers to his feet. "Where the heck am I?" he asks, not sounding overly concerned. He seems altogether much happier than before the sleeping gas. He gazes up at the towering redwoods, looming in the ranger's flashlight beam. "These trees are exceptional. Such incredible beauty! And it smells delightful in here. Am I dreaming? Perhaps I'm dreaming. But what an amazing dream! *Look* at these trees!" He hops from one foot to the other, brimming over with excitement.

The ranger sighs. "Never a dull moment," she says to herself. "Okay, folks, it's time to go. Park is closed. Get moving. Stay close. Don't want to lose anyone on the way out." She slides a hand under Slack's arm to guide him back up the trail. The couple follows the ranger and we follow the couple.

We let our new companions get a bit ahead so we can talk without being overheard. But what to say? Waves of sadness wash over me. I can see Albert as the rip closed behind him. My heart, which is all kinds of smashed, presses against my chest. How can I feel like I've lost everything but gained so much at the same time? These two things should not coexist.

"Are you okay, Cassie?" Joe asks.

I shake my head. No. Tears make hot little trails down my cheeks.

But while I'm not okay now, I think I *will* be. Back when I climbed into that dumpster and found Albert, I never would have guessed I could do all the things I've done since then. Dad was right. The universe doesn't like quitters. And it keeps testing me, throwing things and knocking me down. But I keep getting up.

I'm still *here*.

Chapter 35

THE UNEXPECTED

BY THE TIME WE REACH the trailhead parking lot, my tears are mostly dried, my feet are completely soaked, and my hands are numb. Picking our way through the creek in the fern canyon, over rocks and downed trees, was no joke. When Joe slipped off a log and into freezing water up to his knees, he reminded me that this is the very reason he is not outdoorsy. It is cold and miserable and the opposite of fun. A steady drizzle begins. The dragon might be gone, but Lewiston's weather still stinks.

There are four cars parked side by side in the small trailhead lot. One is green and white and belongs to the park ranger. One is a rusted old van, with faded rainbow decals on the rear windows. I guess this belongs to the hikers. It has that vibe to it. The other two cars are nondescript blue sedans.

The boring blue cars belong to Agent Fox and Agent Dana. Am I surprised to find them here? Not really. They stride toward us with purpose.

"I'm Agent Fox and this is Agent Dana." Agent Fox smiles at the ranger, but there is no warmth behind her eyes.

"I know who you are," the ranger says, narrowing her gaze. "I've heard of you. You've been to our woods before."

"Indeed we have," Agent Dana says.

"So what I think I saw fly overhead," the ranger says slowly, "might actually *be* what I thought I saw fly overhead?"

Agent Fox gazes at the ranger. "We'd like to thank you for your help here tonight," she says evenly.

The ranger does not seem surprised by the evasion, but it doesn't make her happy. "These are my woods," she mutters. "It would be nice if I was clued in." No one thinks to bring us up to speed, and I get the distinct feeling questions will not be welcome.

Agent Fox steps up to Sheldon Slack, who is still looking all around him as if he has never been in the woods before, as if life, the universe, and everything is just *so* wonderful. That sleeping gas has really short-circuited his wiring.

"Sheldon," Agent Fox says. Slack grins like a dope. Agent Dana frowns. "We thought we'd come to an understanding last time. That you were going to steer clear of things related to . . . well . . . I think you know."

Slack, for his part, struggles to figure out who these people are and what they are talking about and why he should care. He keeps smiling, although his eyes begin to register a low level of concern. Or maybe he's just realizing that he's soaking wet, muddy, and cold, with no memory of how he got here.

"Do we know each other?" he asks cautiously.

Agent Dana sighs. "Okay, let's go." She takes Slack by the shoulders and gently maneuvers him to one of the blue cars. "I'm going to take you home now."

"Home?" he replies. "Wonderful! Um . . . where exactly might that be?"

Oh boy.

Agent Fox turns to the rest of us. She gives the hikers a quick up-and-down, taking their measure. They visibly recoil under her gaze. It is that intense, even in the semi-darkness.

"The best thing," Agent Fox says, "would be for you two to

hit the road. We'll overlook the broken taillight, the lapsed vehicle registration, and the fact that you blew through a four-way stop sign yesterday in downtown Lewiston."

The hikers glance at each other. How does this person know about the stop sign? Who is she? But they get the message loud and clear.

"Right," the woman says. "Don't have to ask us twice." They scurry off to their van before Agent Fox changes her mind, and then who knows what would happen? They don't want to find out.

Agent Fox turns her gaze on the park ranger next. "I've got it from here," she says.

"I figured," replies the ranger. She offers a casual salute and she, too, heads to her car. Moments later, three sets of taillights bump down the washboard dirt road and disappear into the night. Now it is just us and Fox, in the dark, in the middle of the woods. My hands move automatically to my hoodie pocket, but Albert is gone, and what if I can only be brave when he is with me?

"Children," Agent Fox says. I bet she was never a kid, not even when she was young. She has that sharp look to her. "Listen very carefully. There has been a lot of excitement here in Lewiston, and I want to be sure we are on the same page about what *actually* happened. If the wrong story is allowed to circulate, things can get complicated, and that wouldn't be good for anyone. Agreed?"

I glance at Joe. He doesn't know where this is going either.

"Sheldon Slack," Agent Fox continues, "is well known to us. He suffers from ideas that are not necessarily grounded in reality."

Now, let me be clear. I'm no fan of Sheldon Slack, but he was right about dragons existing. I mean, how does Agent Fox think we got here in the first place?

Agent Fox cuts me off before my questions can tumble out. "Whatever you think you experienced, you *didn't*. And just to be clear, there are *consequences* for saying otherwise."

There is a word for when someone tries to convince you that your memories or perceptions aren't true, that what you *know* happened didn't. If they do it for long enough and consistently enough, you start to question the facts. You might even start to believe you are losing your marbles. It's on the tip of my tongue.

Gaslighting.

And to make matters worse, Agent Fox has thrown the threat of consequences on top to keep us in line. Otherwise she cannot say what will happen. We will probably end up being disappeared into the night like Sheldon

Slack. Because I'm pretty sure they aren't just giving him a lift home.

Beside me, Joe goes very still. "Now, confirm that you hear what I'm saying," Agent Fox says. "That you understand."

There is no room for negotiation. The best thing we can do is agree with Agent Fox. I'm not sure we even have a choice.

"No dragon," I say quietly.

"Very good," Agent Fox says, turning to Joe. "And you?"

"No dragon," Joe replies quickly.

"Well, that certainly was easy," Agent Fox says, satisfied. "I'll take you home now. I'm sure you are exhausted. As the ranger said, hiking at night can be dangerous. At the very least, you want to bring a flashlight."

As we drive, Agent Fox offers up details of events that didn't happen. We took a bus to the woods. We'd heard the rumors about the fairies and the full moon. What happened in Mia's bedroom was all just a big misunderstanding that has been addressed. Sheldon Slack was another situation entirely. Unrelated in any way to us. We can relax. We are safe now. Everything is fine. Adventure over.

"One hundred percent insane," Joe mouths from the seat beside me.

The car pulls to the curb at Joe's house first. His entire

family—his parents, and all those brothers—pile out the front door and smother him as soon as he steps foot on the sidewalk. There is a lot of yelling and shouting. Agent Fox tells me to sit tight. I watch her outside, talking to Joe's parents, relief rolling off them in waves as they nod and agree. Is she telling them the same story she told us? They don't seem to doubt her at all. I wish I could talk to Joe. I wish Albert were here.

My house is next. My mother hovers in the door, dressed in real clothes for the first time in months, jeans and a red flannel shirt. Her hair is pulled back into a tight ponytail, so I can see her face clearly. And it's *awake*, just like the other day. I'm not even out of the car before she throws herself at me.

"Cassie," she whispers into my hair. "I thought I lost you, too. I thought I was too late." She hugs me so hard, my lungs go flat. "I don't want to be too late."

"Mom, you're squishing me," I murmur, but the truth is I don't want her to let go. It has been a long time since she has hugged me tightly like this.

Agent Fox waits patiently until Mom releases me, wiping her eyes. My mother seems not only awake but present, like she is fully here all of a sudden. "Agent Fox," she says evenly. "I don't know how to thank you."

I look from Mom to Agent Fox, trying to figure out who knows what. There is an undercurrent of tension.

"Just doing our job, Mrs. Jones," Agent Fox replies. "As I briefed you earlier, everything has been resolved. Just a number of unrelated events seeming to converge and complicate what were otherwise several discrete situations." Huh? What do those words even *mean*?

"Cassie is safe," Mom says. "That's all that matters." She pulls me in to the crook of her hip, wrapping her arm around my waist.

Agent Fox levels a gaze at me. "You and your friend were very brave," she says. "But in a day or two, it will be like it never happened. I'm certain."

Sure she is, because we've been warned what happens if we don't conveniently "forget." *Consequences.* "Yeah," I say. "Got it." Sheldon Slack is probably in one kind of prison and I'm in another. Suddenly overcome with fatigue, I slump against Mom.

"I'm going to get Cassie to bed," Mom says, moving toward the front door. "Good night, Agent Fox."

"Right," she says, gazing at us. "I'll keep an eye on you. Just to make sure everything is okay."

Her words are benign, courteous, even, but the threat is clear. My head swims as Mom leads me up the stairs. I want to tell her everyone is lying. I want to tell her the fairy story is complete nonsense, that Albert is a real dragon but he's gone. I was prepared to be grilled and questioned and disbelieved and interrogated, but I never expected *this*. I wonder if over on the national park streets Joe is having the same experience. My reality and the reality presented by Agent Fox do not align. It makes my head hurt.

"Come on, honey." Mom holds my hand as we climb the stairs, as if she is afraid I will get lost. My legs feel like lead. My heart aches. The empty hoodie pouch feels vast like the ocean. The world is upside down.

But there, sitting on my bed, her spiky hair all the colors of the rainbow, is none other than Miss Asher.

"We have a lot to talk about," she says.

Chapter 36

AND HOW IT BEGINS AGAIN

MISS ASHER'S PRESENCE in my room surprises me, and, quite honestly, I thought by this point I was beyond surprise.

"What are you doing here?" I blurt. I look to Mom, who gives me a faint smile.

"Ellen came here after the incident on the roof," Mom says. It's weird to hear Miss Asher called by her first name, even if Mom was once her teacher. "After Albert flew off with you and your friend Joe."

This puts me back on my heels. "You *know* about Albert?" I ask.

"I've known Ellen for a long time," Mom says. "No

student was ever as curious or eager to investigate and understand. I remember having to throw her out of the science lab just so I could go home at night."

Miss Asher smiles at this memory.

"It's why she is the world's best librarian," Mom continues. "When Agent Fox and Agent Dana showed up here asking questions and telling me some story about you guys going rogue and hunting woodland fairies . . . well . . . I just had this feeling like something wasn't right. It started with you saying you fell off a skateboard. I should have asked more questions, and I'm sorry I didn't. But that was the first moment in so long I felt the universe talking to me. It really woke me up." She runs a hand down my hair, her fingers getting caught up in the knots. "And as Dad liked to say, when the universe is trying to tell you something, you had better listen."

Mom gestures to my bedroom, all the burn marks and the piles of ash that used to be socks and a few scattered glittery scales. It is also the first time I've heard her reference my father in a way not bound in despair. Mom makes a sandwich of my hands in hers.

"I'm sorry you couldn't tell me," Mom says. "I'm sorry I've been gone for so long. But I'm working hard to be here now and to stay here. And I promise you I won't quit."

I don't want to burst into tears, but I do anyway. This person in jeans and flannel sounds like Mom. She looks like Mom, and suddenly I'm keenly aware of how I've missed her. It's as if Albert's parting gift was to give her back to me. She hugs me and whispers into my hair while Miss Asher studies her manicure, which is ten different colors.

When I finally stop, Miss Asher pats the bed next to her, and I take a seat. "Where's Albert?" she asks quietly.

"He's gone," I reply.

"That's good," she says, nodding her head thoughtfully. "Did he go out over the ocean? Or did he fly north? Did he leave you with any sense of where he was headed? I'd think the wilderness of Canada, being so extensive, would be perfect."

"No," I respond. "You don't understand. We opened a *rip*, and he went home. Back to his world."

Miss Asher's face turns pale. "He *what*?"

"He couldn't stay here," I explain. "It was hurting him. And then Sheldon showed up trying to kidnap him. He just could never be safe here."

Mom strokes my cheek. "He's so lucky you found him," she says. "It's okay."

But the look in Miss Asher's eyes tells me that it is not. "I don't understand," I say slowly. "He went *home*."

Miss Asher inhales sharply. "You never got to the part in my journal about the mark, did you?"

"The what?" Despite being exhausted, my heart begins to accelerate, fueled by pure adrenaline.

"The *prophecy*," she says. And I remember the prediction that a dragon would come to overthrow the ruling Silvers, ending their reign. And this dragon would be *marked*.

"What is the mark?" I whisper, somehow knowing the answer yet not wanting to hear it.

"The dragon of the prophecy will bear a golden blaze," Miss Asher says. "Albert was somehow hidden here—I'm sure of it—by his mother or his family or someone. It was to *protect* him so Vayne could not get to him."

My legs quiver, and I sit down hard next to Miss Asher, the full meaning of her words taking shape.

"Why would he go back if he knew what was waiting?" I cry.

"He would not have known," Miss Asher ventures. "He would have been too young to understand. His mother would have sent him away as soon as she could, an act of last resort."

But the reasons don't matter. It is all the same in the end. I have sent my cat, my dragon, back to an almost-certain death. "What have I done?" I whisper, burying my face in my hands. A deep, cold fear churns in my stomach.

Albert, how do I save you?

I desperately want to hear that voice in my head, the one I am sure is him, telling me exactly what I need to do, giving me hope.

My mother gasps.

"Cassie!" I look up to see I am surrounded by a cloud of glittery light. A sphere of sparkles rises from my upturned palms. It is the same iridescent glow that rose from Albert's golden blaze when he opened the rip. I gaze at it with wonder.

Miss Asher takes one of my hands in hers. "This is what happened at the rip?" she asks, eyes wide.

I nod. I remember hugging Albert, putting my palms to the golden blaze. "Yes," I say. "It was just like this." A sparkly fog, the massive trees bending down, the rain and the wind. It felt like all the energy of the forest was with us, focused on that tiny space, the doorway between two worlds.

I see it on Miss Asher's face, and Mom's, before the thought is even fully formed in my own head. I glance down at my hands, and I know what we have to do. We have to *save* Albert. It doesn't matter if the universe is on my side. I can do hard things. And while I sense Albert is okay right now, at this moment, I do not know how long that will last. We have to go through the rip and get him.

Joe is going to *love* this. Just wait until I tell him the adventure isn't over.

In fact, it is just *beginning*.

Acknowledgments

This story came to me while I was having coffee with my black cat. She joins me most mornings, standing on the counter and generally being a nuisance, getting super irritated with me when I don't tend to her needs (which are mostly about food) immediately. I was petting her on the head, telling her to be patient, when I squished back her ears—if you have a cat, you may know what I'm talking about—and that is when it hit me. She looked exactly like a *dragon*! A tiny fluffy dragon with a spectacular tail, but still a dragon.

Afterward, all I could think was *What if my cat is a dragon?* I could see a number of problems with that being true, like she'd burn down the house or fly through the roof and things, but I also thought it was awesome. I called my brother because he loved a good story and was always someone I ran ideas by when they were just hatched, fresh, new, and full of possibility. His reaction was a good indication as to whether the idea might have legs. This one, he liked.

Secret of the Storm, written almost entirely in quarantine, during one of the hardest years of my life, is for him. He never got to read it, but somehow, somewhere, by the magic that is imagination, I believe he knows how it goes.

Happy reading, my friends.

About the Author

BETH McMULLEN is the author of the Mrs. Smith's Spy School for Girls series; the Lola Benko, Treasure Hunter series, and several adult mysteries. Her books have mighty girls, messy situations, really bad bad guys, action, adventure, thrills, chills, and laughs.

An avid reader, she once missed her subway stop and rode the train all the way to Brooklyn because the book she was reading was that good.

She lives in Northern California with her family; two cats; and a parakeet named Zeus, who is sick of the cats eyeballing him like he's dinner.

Visit her at BethMcMullenBooks.com.